# Watch th

# Watch the Birdie

### The Life and Times of
### Richard and Cherry Kearton,
### Pioneers of Nature Photography

Richard Kearton

# W R Mitchell

CASTLEBERG
2001

## For Marie

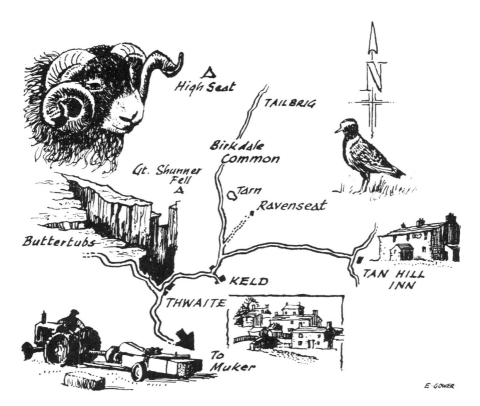

KEARTON COUNTRY

A **Castleberg** Book.

First published in the United Kingdom in 2001.

Text, © W R Mitchell 2001.

The moral right of the author has been asserted.

ISBN 1 871064 34 1

Typeset in Garamond, printed and bound in the United Kingdom by Lamberts Print & Design, Station Road, Settle, North Yorkshire, BD24 9AA.

Published by Castleberg, 18 Yealand Avenue, Giggleswick, Settle, North Yorkshire, BD24 0AY.

# Contents

# Foreword

### by Martin Withers
### *(Hon Sec of the Zoological Photographic Club)*

A SIMPLE image depicting the nest and eggs of a Song Thrush, produced by the Kearton brothers on April 11, 1892, is considered to be one of the first bird photographs. Over the course of thirty years, Richard and Cherry Kearton pioneered photographic techniques and provided answers to many of the problems posed by nature photography.

Some of their field techniques, such as the use of hides, are still practised by today's exponents of the art of nature photography. The brothers produced numerous books and a plethora of magazine articles that brought to the attention of the public at large the beauty and wealth of nature around us and acted as a catalyst for what is today the world-wide conservation movement.

The work of the Keartons and other notable pioneers has been represented in the postal portfolios of the Zoological Photographic Club, of which Richard was a member for two periods from 1909 until his death in 1928. The Club, founded in 1899, was the first of its kind and the postal portfolios are still circulated today within a selected membership.

A book specifically chronicling the lives and times of these remarkable brothers is long overdue. The volume you now hold in your hands is a fine tribute to these pioneers of nature photography and will be cherished by photographers and historians alike.

# An Overview

MY INTRODUCTION to the Kearton brothers came when, as a small boy living in the sooty world of a Yorkshire milltown, I borrowed a copy of *With Nature and a Camera*, first published in 1897, and read with mounting excitement of their visit to St Kilda, a scatter of Scottish islands. So vivid was the bonding of words and photographs, I felt able to join them on a great adventure that began when they left the Clyde in an old steamboat and sailed through stormy waters to the haven of Village Bay.

For half a century I retained mental pictures of St Kilda – of a self-reliant "bird people", dependent on seafowl for much of their food, for feathers to be used for bedding or barter and for the oil that kept their lamps burning during the long northern winter. Fifty years after I read of the Keartons' stormy passage to St Kilda, having just retired, with a fortnight to spare, I crossed to the archipelago on water as calm as the proverbial mill-pond as a member of a working party organised by the National Trust for Scotland. In almost every conscious minute, during that fortnight "at the edge of the world", the Keartons were with me in spirit.

As editor of *The Dalesman* magazine, I kept a finger on the pulse of Dales life and frequently crossed the Buttertubs Pass from Wensleydale to Thwaite, in upper Swaledale, where they were born and reared. The end cottage grandly known as Corner House was distinctive because the owner, J G Reynoldson, a retired builder, had the lintel carved with the outlines of birds and beasts known to Richard and Cherry Kearton. George, their cousin and childhood playmate, used to tell of their boyish escapades, adding: "Aye, an' I mind too that Dicky [Richard Kearton] were a rare 'un at gudlin' [tickling] trout."

Richard and Cherry Kearton's main claim to distinction is that they produced the first nature book to be illustrated throughout by authentic photographs of wildlife. They were by no means the first to photograph a wild bird. When, in 1892, the brothers took their first "picture direct from nature", and decided to write a book, with Richard as author and Cherry as photographer, a chemist named Benjamin Wyles had photographed gulls in flight above Southport pier. He had also been to the Farne Islands, off the Northumbrian coast, to photograph the teeming seabird life. His best pictures were featured in *The Strand* magazine under the heading *The Camera Amongst the Seabirds*.

R B Lodge, of Enfield, was portraying the bird life of his locality. His brother George helped to transport a 12 x 10 inch plate camera on a wheelbarrow. Lodge and a younger man, Oliver G Pike, experimented with trip-wires placed near nests by which birds could photograph themselves.

The Kearton brothers, employees of Cassell, one of the world's big publishers, saw their opportunity to do something distinctive when an American invented a process for half-tone reproduction of photographs. The tones were translated into dots, of uniform tone but varying sizes. Previously, book illustrations had been in the form of engravings. Richard Kearton became a notable lecturer in the days of "magic" lanterns and tinted slides. He believed in "teaching through the eye".

As an early conservationist, keen to discourage the random collection of the eggs of rare birds, he asserted that the weakest living thing on the face of the earth has its right. He wished "some epicure would try a boiled rook egg for breakfast and proclaim from the house-tops of Belgravia its superiority over that of the plover or lapwing, which is being slowly but surely exterminated." Richard foresaw that the struggle for existence would become keener and that "our future men and women will require to turn more to Nature and her children for health and recreation."

Cherry was one of the first naturalists to use a telephoto lens and almost certainly the first man to film London from the air. He went globe-trotting with his movie-camera, describing his experiences in several well-illustrated books and he enthralled audiences with the first films of African wildlife. He attempted to record the song of a nightingale on a wax disc, using one of Mr Edison's machines (the bird was put off singing by the hiss of the needle on the waxed drum and resumed as soon as the instrument was switched off). Richard, with the help of his daughter Grace, continued to portray wildlife in a popular way. A book published in 1915 contained 72 photographs, several having been reproduced in acceptable colour.

Snippets about the Keartons have appeared in many published works, not least their own. Now they have a book to themselves. Its compilation has been made possible through the interest and help of members of the family: Marguerite Bentham and Primrose Razell (Richard's granddaughters), Cherry Kearton (grandson), Jean Brown (nee Kearton) and Mrs J Wilshaw. Some family history was derived from *Yorkshire and Yonder; families of Keartons*, by Basil Kearton of New Zealand, published in 1995. The author had a helpful chat with Marie Hartley, Dales writer and artist.

While every attempt was made to trace the copyright holders of photographs taken by the two brothers, if copyright has been unwittingly violated, apologies are extended to the holders, who should contact the author. Cassell, who published so much of their work, had insufficient information in their records to grant or refuse permission so where appropriate mention has been made of the books in which photographs appeared. Marguerite Bentham and Cherry Kearton were willing for the author to use photographs not otherwise covered by copyright. He was grateful to Mrs Wilshaw for permission to copy prints of the family from her album. Uncredited line drawings are by E. Jeffrey. The colour photograph of a red grouse on the front cover was taken by Colin Preston, FRPS, and is reproduced with his kind permission.

Interestingly, three acres of farmland near Thwaite are still owned by direct descendants of Richard and Cherry Kearton. The family has thus retained its little stake in the Yorkshire Dales. On completion of this book, the author intends to donate his extensive Kearton material to the J B Priestley Library of the University of Bradford, to join the W R Mitchell Archive, one of the special collections.

W R MITCHELL.

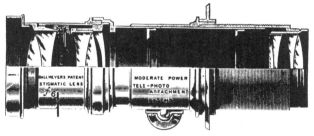

# Meet the Keartons

A BRANCH of the Kearton family living at Ivelet combined farming with lead-mining and had their children baptised at Gunnerside by the Catholic priest who travelled up the dale from Richmond. Through their religion they were in fellowship with small enclaves. George Kearton, born in 1762, left Ivelet for London where he became a cheesemonger. Settling down with a young lady in unwedded bliss, he became the father of a daughter, Nancy Wells Kearton, who inherited most of his wealth. He did make provision for members of his immediate family who remained in Swaledale.

The Keartons of Thwaite, from which sprang the celebrated naturalists, Richard and Cherry, were small-time farmers and ardent Wesleyans. The occurrence of Cherry as a Christian name in each generation dates back to the middle of the eighteenth century, when a Kearton married a Cherry. This was the name bestowed on the grandfather of the brothers, a Methodist local preacher with a sunny disposition and the massive, simple faith of the dalesman. On hearing a report of the sudden death of his best cow, he cheerily exclaimed: "The Lord giveth and the Lord taketh away, glory be unto His name." He meant every word of it. Grandfather was a small-time farmer who did some game-watching on the moors. Organised poaching called for the utmost vigilance, but grandfather never fired a gun in his life except by accident and that to the detriment of a rackful of plates in the kitchen.

His son John (usually referred as a Hack) married Jane Miller. They begat two daughters, Jane and Margaret, and three sons – Richard, Cherry and Foster – of whom Richard was to begin his autobiography with the words: "I was born on Jan 2, 1862, at Thwaite in Swaledale, a pretty valley running like a cart-wheel rut between the silent fells of the Pennine Range… I come of yeoman stock and, I imagine, possess a fair share of the vices and virtues of that sturdy folk." His first recollection of life at Thwaite was of the "proud day" when he changed his petticoats for knickers and a wee jacket. "My sex was established beyond cavil and I strutted round our village as proud as a peacock." The newly-breeched boy showed himself to relatives and friends, who filled his little pockets with coppers.

His brother Foster became a dare-devil with a reputation of "stopping at nowt". On a wet day, when he had been feeding sheep on the fell, he set off for home on his pony, only to discover heavy rain had brought the beck out in flood. The pony jibbed. Foster is said to have lifted up its front legs, placing them over his shoulder so that he might drag the pony through the foaming water.

When the Kearton children were young, Thwaite was visibly suffering from the close of lead-mining and was in part ruinous. Its genesis was during the Norse colonisation, the name of the village being derived from *thveit*, meaning a clearing, presumably in the ancient forest. The canny Norse named what became known as Great Shunnor Fell from *sjon* and *sjonar*, meaning a look-out hill. Richard and Cherry had this great hill and the "island hill" known as Kisdon as a backdrop to their early lives.

Richard and Cherry were to absorb much of their knowledge of wildlife from grandfather. He was also fond of beck-fishing and, aged over eighty and with failing eyesight, he persuaded young Richard to tie some scarlet wool just above the first "dropper" so that he might know when his fishing flies were in the water." Uncle George, known to the dalesfolk as Cher Dawd, was a brawny chap who flung a heavy shawl over one shoulder when he went out and about to wage war against poachers who plagued the moors around Swaledale.

The Kearton farm consisted of sixteen acres of meadowland and eighteen acres of rough pasture, with grazing rights on Thwaite

Common. Father was also gamekeeper of sorts to a Mr Brookes of Huddersfield and therefore took more than a passing interest in natural history. Under his guidance, it was not long before Richard "knew where to find the nest of every species breeding in our neighbourhood and to distinguish the cry of any feathered friend almost as soon as it was uttered." Richard played the usual boyish pranks with his brothers. They dropped peats down old women's chimneys. When his mother made a cake, he surreptitiously spooned out the inside before replacing the top.

Their knowledge was acquired from life, not books. "In our boyhood days among the solitary Yorkshire moors we dated the coming and going of the swallows; were chastised for attempting to lie out all night in order to see the owner of a curiously shaped bird's nest return to it in the morning, and thereby discover the species to which it belonged." When Cherry went out and about with Richard, his elder brother, they carried feathers from the chicken run to a bridge spanning a beck, "where we dropped them for the swallows to catch as they flew underneath." Richard noted: "We invested all our slender stock of pocket-money in a thermometer by which to find out the relationship between the temperature of neighbouring streams and the variation in the spawning time of the trout living in them; noted the flocking of female chaffinches in the winter; and learnt to imitate the call-notes of most of the wild creatures inhabiting the hills around our home."

Mother paid for Richard to attend a dame school run by the wife of a village cobbler. A naughty child was tied to the leg of a table by a piece of white cotton thread and severely lectured in front of the other children. Richard and another lad, who misbehaved, were banished to an unlighted coal-cellar where they amused themselves by pushing handfuls of small coals through a notch-hole in the door on to the floor of a spotlessly clean passage beyond. Having unfastened a trapdoor barring the hole through which coals were shovelled on delivery, they were soon rid of school and engaged in the cleaner pastime of tickling bullheads in the local beck.

When Richard was seven, his education was retarded by a serious accident. While climbing a tree to reach a nest, he fell heavily, severely damaging his left hip, and was taken along the moorland road to Kirkby Stephen, in Westmorland, where there was known to be a bone-setter. This worthy operated on the lad at a rural inn after drinking eight glasses of brandy. He was assisted by ex-harvest men, both of whom were drunk. They restrained Richard during the operation. There was no anaesthetic to dull his senses.

"He made me much worse. It all ended in my becoming a permanent cripple – and a field naturalist." Richard now had one leg several inches shorter than the other. The difference was compensated for when a thick cork sole was attached to his left boot. Although he remained quite active, he was also content with sitting and staring. Hence his remarkable knowledge of the activities of birds and beasts.

At the age of eight, Richard stood up in Muker church and answered questions by which he earned Lord Wharton's Bible Prize. He was to proudly claim that his paternal grandmother was a descendant of the once-powerful Wharton family, the last head of which was Philip, Lord Wharton, who had instituted and endowed the Gift Bible scheme.

In his boyhood, Richard led a Huckleberry Finn kind of existence, wandering "happy and hungry" from one trout stream to another, having made a fishing rod from rowan, with a line made of freshly-plucked horse-hair. He was an expert at tickling trout, carefully working his hand beside a boulder to stroke the body of a fish and then adroitly grasping it and with a single vigorous motion tossing it on to dry land. Richard described the process as "grobbing". He was often content to lie on sunbaked stones and peer into a pool where trout had gathered.

He was to recall that "a little way below the funnel hole the river meanders over a shingle bank and tumbles into another deep pool crowded with trout of all ages and sizes. In droughty weather you can see them through the six or seven feet of limpid water all lying at rest, like a regiment of soldiers, every head pointing upstream. In these congregations the small fish are compelled to keep an ever-wary eye on the larger ones, because old trout have a disagreeable habit of turning cannibal.

"I have seen, nay caught, in the days of my youth, when tickling was not regarded as poaching and trout far more plentiful than in these by-law-bound times, a fish a foot and a half long with another in its mouth so large it could not be swallowed and had to be digested piecemeal. A hungry, unsophisticated trout will rise at anything he can swallow... I tickled a pounder from beneath the dark recesses of an overhanging bank and discovered he had just sucked down an innocent little water shrew as he swam across a pool no wider than the surface of an ordinary-sized dining table."

He recalled dippers that bred safely "on the upper edge of a damp, unapproachable slope of an overhung rock and quite above the high-water mark of anything but an abnormal flood. If you attempted to swim to it across the pool, the chances are you would not be able to scramble up its steep, slippery side, and might be sucked to destruction by the volume of water dragging for ever downwards towards a hole in the lower rim." Nesting a few yards overhead, in a small inaccessible crevice, was the grey wagtail, a bird with "a canary yellow breast and long, black tail."

Swale and Eden rise close to each other. Richard grew up at a time when the upper Eden Valley was rich in bird life. "Picture to yourself a few acres of more or less flat ground... besprinkled with tufts of rushes and encroaching patches of bracken, with here and there a

moss-grown boulder peeping out in forlorn isolation… Through the
middle the river meanders, a mere trickle shining in the sunlight like
a snail's silvery trail, wearing away when in spate first one bank then
the other, making excellent breeding-places for innumerable sand
martins that skim and twirl over its pools and ripply shallows… and
you will be able to visualise the headquarters of the sandpiper and
yellow wagtails in the months of May and June."

As a lad, Richard teased rabbits. He would lie in a dry ditch near
a wood swarming with rabbits and when fifty or sixty had ventured
out into the field would squeal out in imitation of one being killed –
just to see them bound away.

Muker

# Brothers to the Ox

RICHARD was almost seventeen when he left Muker School to become a farmhand and a shepherd. He had the saddening experience of overhearing his parents discussing the future of their children. "Jane'll go into service, Jack'll go on to farm; Richard – he's lame – he'll do nowt." Farming, which was primarily a handcraft, "toughened the steel in my character".

The Keartons had a modest acreage of their own and two small farms rented from different landlords. The man who owned the larger plot of the two was Owd Bob, who was utterly mean, "the sort of man who would gladly have made a shirt stud out of a wart growing on the back of his neck or charged a blind spider a halfpenny for the body of a dead fly." By trying to cheat his cows, when he farmed the place himself, the mean old rascal had turned a coarse but fairly sound pasture into a quivering bog. When one sat down in it to milk a cow, the legs of the stool sank out of sight and very nearly the same fate overtook those of the luckless animals. It was impossible to get an ordinary milk-can under a cow. It had to be gripped between the knees of the husbandman and the milk squirted into it at an angle of about forty-five degrees."

Richard's father threatened to give the place up altogether unless the pasture was drained. Owd Bob grudgingly consented – with special conditions. The Keartons would have to do the work. And Bob would be paid, on his outlay, interest at the rate of five per cent per annum. During Bob's last illness, his housekeeper sat up and nursed him. Even when near the end, he asked her to blow out the tallow dip burning on a little table by his bedside in order to save the expense. As there was no other light in the room she flatly refused to do this. "Not having enough breath left in his frail body to do it himself, the old sinner raised the corner of the quilt, flicked it out and chuckled gleefully over his success. A few hours after this he was dead."

In November, just before tupping time, and before the onset of the long Pennine winter, Richard helped to apply salve to the skins of the animals, shedding wool in rows and stroking the bared flesh with fingers holding a blend of Norway tar and Irish butter. His basic accomplishment was in helping to make "a couple of nourishing blades of grass grow where only one struggled for existence before." Kearton land edged up to the Buttertubs Pass, which was named after limestone shafts, some sixty feet deep. Richard watched with admiration as his elder brother descended one of the shafts on a rope.

Farm life was ill-rewarded. About 1879, when there was sheep rot, Richard's father sent him to a fair in the following autumn with some of the lambs. "They were such a poor lot, he told me that if I could not dispose of them at any price, to leave them on the roadside. He didn't want to see them about the place any more. I sold them at three shillings and sixpence each, which was all they were worth." Brother Cherry enjoyed bringing in the moorland sheep. "Sometimes a mist would creep over the mountains and then, knowing that I could not find my way home, I would sit down and watch the sheep: they always fed in the direction of home. I had then only to keep in that direction, getting a fresh guide whenever I felt in danger of once more losing the way." There were ravens in remote parts of the fells and, as ever, the plovers – tewits and golden plovers – infusing life into the wilds with their plaintive calls.

The winters were long, hard and dark. In January, 1881, a blizzard raged. Richard left home before daylight to look for overblown sheep. He returned after dark. His two sheepdogs were so tired they could scarcely crawl after him. In about 1879, when there was an outbreak of foot rot, the sheep died so fast they had to be buried in trenches. "Those that did not die did worse, for they consumed a lot of good fodder and never paid for it."

There was black-magic about some local beliefs when faced with illness in animals. Some men would not move their cattle from one shippon to another on a Friday because the day was considered unlucky and a cow would accidentally neck itself on the band that loosely tethered it. A farmer or one of his family with whooping cough was tempted to follow the old idea and eat a roasted mouse. Superstitious folk believe that if the mattress was filled with pigeon rather than goose feathers no-one would die while sleeping on it.

A farmer forced a live trout down a heifer's throat in the belief that "the trout had the power to make cattle breed". His belief was justified in this case. She bore a calf in the following spring. The cure for an adder's bite was "to rush to the nearest stream and take a drink of water" the belief being that the snake was sure to do so and if it beat the man it had bitten he would die. If he managed to get there first, the adder would perish in his stead.

# Moorcock and Men

THE KEARTONS were "moor birds". George Kearton (nick-named Cher) erected a small building on Gunnerside Pasture from which to watch out for poachers. Long after his watchtower had degenerated into a heap of stones it was known as Cher Currack. One of Richard's forebears, a man of strong religious faith, was teasingly invited by a party of visiting sportsmen to express that faith in prayer. The old chap knelt down by a boulder and, wrote Richard, "instead of offering the gibing company something to laugh at, he soon had everyone in tears."

The moors above Swaledale were a resort of sheep and red grouse. Heather, the staple food of grouse, clung to the dry spots, keeping its feet out of water. When they had eaten and the shrubby stuff was being processed in a special gut, the grouse sat among the heather tufts to cheat the wind and bequeathed to the land their bright green, pencil-shaped droppings. A hen bird, taking a brief respite from brooding a clutch of eggs, left a single huge dropping, known to the gamekeepers as a "clocking foil".

Peat which dry winds eroded into curious mushroom-shaped forms had been laid down over many centuries and consisted of plant life that, in the absence of oxygen, had compacted into layers, some of them being as dark and hard as coal. The moor-edge farmers had turbary rights, which meant they could cut peat to be stacked and used as winter fuel. In the peat bogs were pickled traces of past plant life, even pieces of birch from ancient woodland. Now one could see a mosaic of plants tolerant to acid conditions, notably sphagnum moss which, used by humans for wounds, was sterile and absorbent to the nasty elements.

On some moors, waste heaps from lead-mining were like huge grey carbuncles. The great-grandfather of Richard and Cherry dabbled in mining and – wrote Richard – "trusting to his limited knowledge of geology, engaged an army of miners to delve a neighbouring hill-side after glittering ore, but alas! Whenever matters looked at all encouraging he would celebrate by releasing spates of gin amongst his men and my great-grandmother never saw the silk frocks and prancing carriage horses he promised her."

For most of the year, the only visitors to the moors were small-time farmers and gamekeepers. The last-named were responsible for the controlled burning of rank heather. Clouds of smoke rose like incense into the air on still days towards the end of winter and soon new growth was evident, food for grouse and sheep. Gamekeepers also kept down the "vermin" – crows, stoats, foxes and poachers.

Nothing must unduly disturb the sacred grouse so that on the Glorious Twelfth of August they would be present in abundance when the gentry arrived to ritualistically cull them. The normally lack-lustre moorland was by then overspread with purple as the bonnie heather bloomed. In dry weather, as the "guns" walked towards the butts, boots were dusted white with pollen from the ling.

Generations of Keartons had a reverence for the moors. Richard and Cherry would hear tales of old-time sportsmen using muzzle-loading guns who shot grouse over dogs. The dogs ranged ahead and "pointed" when they detected grouse, which were then flushed and despatched. Another ploy was to fly a kite so that the birds, thinking it was a hawk, remained on the ground until the dogs drew near.

The less sporty custom of grouse-driving came into fashion with the development of breach-loading guns. Curly-coated retrievers were deployed to bring back birds that were slain. Grouse-driving demanded a small army of "beaters" who advanced in a line, sending the coveys of grouse hurtling to where the "guns" were waiting in butts made of peat and heather. Transport to the butts for people and commodities was by horses leased from local farmers. Some grouse, packed in wicker baskets, were transported in Robert Rutter's horse-drawn trap to a game dealer at Richmond.

The Kearton brothers loved the birds, which in spring and summer included a trio of upland waders – golden plover, curlew and peewit, known locally as tewit. At break of day, a moorcock [male grouse] would take flight and then descend on stiffened wings, giving a call – *ka ka ka – ka-ka*. Richard heard the quaint story of an old chap called Birkbeck (locally pronounced Birbeck) who left a nagging wife during the night and trudged off across the moors, with no intention of returning. He was home again shortly after dawn. At first light, the gruff voices of the red grouse sounded to him as though they were shouting: *Birbeck – go back, go back, go back*.

The hen grouse, lighter in tone, had a cryptic colouring to match with the surroundings when she covered her eggs like a feathered tea-cosy. Precocious grouse chicks were soon trying out their stubby wings and by late July had almost reached their adult weight. Game of any kind was predated on by poachers. Lead-miners poached in their spare time at the week-end or even on moonlit nights. It was said that because lead-miners worked in semi-darkness they had especially good night eyes. When there was a full moon, a conscientious gamekeeper would spend hours sitting on the other side of the dale, listening for sounds that might be made by poachers.

The Weardale Gang, composed mainly of lead-miners, were most feared because when they were marauding they had attendant guns and dogs. On the plateau, Height Howe, just east of Crook Seat, stood a watching-house, complete with fireplace. A member of the Kearton family was the watcher [gamekeeper]. It could be a danger-ous occupation, with the possibility of gunshot wounds. The same Kearton was shot in the legs by poachers at another small tower situ-ated at Robert's Seat [locally known as Robersit] on the jagger [pack-horse] route from Raven Seat to Tan Hill.

An annual shepherds' feast, held at Gunnerside from about 1870 until the century's end, was latterly an attempt by the moor-owners to keep the miners sweet and discourage them from wholesale poaching. A meal was the main feature. Two barrels of beer were on tap. Quoits and knur and spell, otherwise known as *batstick*, were favourite sports. Every man was treated to an ounce of tobacco. Gamekeepers were generally contented men. At the turn of last century, John Cherry, gamekeeper, lived at Grain Holme, a good house with an adjacent field in which he kept four cows. His wage for keepering was £1 a week.

# A Dalesman in London

RICHARD'S LIFE was transformed in the early autumn of 1882 when he met Sidney Galpin, a shooting guest of the Huddersfield man who was renting Muker Moor. Sidney was the wealthy son of Thomas Dixon Galpin, who had founded the celebrated London publishing house of Cassell, Petter & Galpin. Accompanying him to Bull Bog, close to the Buttertubs Pass, Richard asked Galpin if he would like him to try his hand at calling up an old cock grouse for him. "He turned to me with what I took to be an expression of incredulity on his face, but consented. We retired to a deep gully in the peat moss and in a few moments I brought along an old moorcock, which was promptly bagged by as pretty a cross shot as I ever saw fired in all my life."

Grouse-calling, known as "becking", was well-known at the time. Gamekeepers used it when culling the oldest cock birds to allow younger ones to occupy the best territories. Poachers preferred it to shooting grouse for obvious reasons. Richard found the call-note of a hen grouse easy to imitate. "It sounds something like *yap, yap, yap* or *yowk, yowk, yowk* and can be reproduced by compressing the nostrils with the index finger and thumb and then emitting the breath in sharp, forced gasps. There are various other methods of calling but by far the most successful is that of sucking quickly at the stem of a clay tobacco-pipe. With the bowl of an ordinary 'churchwarden' and six or seven inches of stem, I would at any time undertake to create such magic sounds as would deceive the most experienced gamekeeper, shepherd or old cock grouse that ever crossed the moor. The great secret of successful 'becking' is to get on to the ground where it can be done before the birds begin to stir in the morning, to keep well out of sight and to call creditably."

Richard's general manner and his ability to call grouse impressed

Galpin. The lame lad had a good head on his shoulders. Galpin asked Richard if he would like "a berth" in London. He would – and did. That October, the "shepherd lad" left Swaledale for the Metropolis. He was set to work in the publicity department of Cassells, addressing envelopes, for which he was paid fourteen shillings a week.

Richard found ground-floor lodgings in a dingy street not far from St John's Gate. "It was the very antithesis of my light and breezy home on the Yorkshire moors." There was neither lock nor bolt on the door of his room. He had to pile furniture behind it to repel intruders before he went to bed. He heard screams at night, also heavy thumps above his head where, it turned out, the police had given chase to a couple of burglars. "In spite of those thrilling happenings I was very lonely – so lonely, in fact, that I used to open the window and let in any stray cat that chanced to come along, to serve as company. While foraging at local coffee-shops for his meals he was appalled by the drunken sordid habits of the London working classes.

At Cassells, from nine to six, he laboured at repetitive work, preferring his workplace to "my miserable abode and its dismal loneliness." When he moved to better quarters in Camberwell, "the sun began to shine again." He made steady upward progress at the firm, especially when someone, taking a fatherly interest in him, paid for him to take a course in Mr Pitman's shorthand at the Birkbeck Institute. Soon he was writing shorthand fast and accurate enough for him to become a clerk and, anxious to improve his vocabulary, he read the leading article in *The Daily Telegraph* daily.

At Cassells, in due course, he was given the task of scanning the daily press for reviews of Cassell publications. He was encouraged to forward ideas for books. The lad from Swaledale became assistant manager of his department and found himself in the stimulating company of such literary luminaries as Oscar Wilde, Sir Philip Gibbs and Sir Arthur Quiller Couch. When his father died in 1887, Richard persuaded his mother to allow his younger brother, Cherry, who was then sixteen years of age, to join the company. His mother and a sister also travelled to London.

Richard developed his writing skills, became a contributor to *Livestock Journal* and then compiled the "nest and eggs" part of Swaysland's *Familiar Wild Birds*, illustrated by Archibald Thorburn and other bird artists, which was to be published in monthly parts. He was paid three guineas for his contribution. The work was never completed. Richard asked if he might finish his own part of the work and see it through the press as a small, separate volume under the title of *Eggs and Egg-Collecting*. This he was allowed to do. The book was published in 1890 and "I received a reward of three guineas for a book now in its nineteenth edition…"

# Pictures from Nature

THE CAREER in bird-photography that was to make the brothers famous began, innocuously, in April, 1892 – when the brothers were staying with some old Yorkshire friends near Enfield. Richard found the nest of a song thrush in what he considered to be a picturesque situation. "I called out to Cherry: 'Here, come and let us see what sort of a fist you can make of this bird's nest with your old sun-picture apparatus'. He did, and the result appeared to me so full of promise that I at once determined to write a book on British birds' nests and illustrate it from beginning to end with photographs taken direct from Nature."

That was the genesis of their natural history photography. Richard wrote the book and Cherry provided the illustrations, observing that "the first photograph, at Enfield, was perhaps the easiest of the lot; for others we had to scale cliffs and lower ourselves over precipices, to scramble on small rocky islands and to climb mountains." The idea for this new form of nature book was not immediately put to Cassells. Instead, Richard posted an illustrated article to a weekly paper as a "feeler". Its prompt acceptance and a request for similar features stimulated the brothers. They laboured, spring by spring, without experience or suggestion, on the pictorial side of their work.

*Birds' Nests*, published in 1895, was the first book of its kind. Dr Bowdler Sharpe of the Natural History Museum proclaimed it as marking a new era in bird study.

When buying a camera, Richard was to recommend putting money into "a lens of good quality and a camera of strength and stability rather than of elegance." The Thornton Pickard half-plate camera used by the brothers was fitted with a Dallmeyer stigmatic lens and an adjustable miniature on the top, used "as a sort of view-finder" when making studies of birds in flight. "When fixed in position and its focus has been set exactly like its working companion beneath it, both are racked out in the same ratio by the screw dominating the larger apparatus which, when charged with a slide and stopped down according to the requirements of light and speed of exposure, needs no further attention."

The photographer focussed the lens with his right hand and, with the left, held the "air-ball or reservoir" of the pneumatic tube used to release the shutter, being squeezed quickly and firmly once the object had been well-defined on the ground-glass of the miniature camera. Richard spoke at length about the virtues of the "silent" shutter on their camera, the shutter being set between the lens and body. Even so there was "a slight grating sound" – enough to make a brooding bird "cock her head on one side in the attitude of listening and, of course, spoil the plate."

For their nature jaunts, Keartons had a good stock of Ilford Chromatic plates, plus a ruby lamp and developing materials. They had a preference for papier-mache trays rather than those made of porcelain "as they are much lighter to take about and less likely to suffer damage at the hands of railway porters." The focussing cloth had been specially made for them of extra large size, being tinted khaki or dead grass brown on one side and "live green grass colour" on the other. "When working inside a stone house or brown earth, or amongst dead grass, we use the khaki side outwards, but when amongst live green grass… the harmonising colour is kept outside." Originally, they weighed down the focussing cloth with "a heavy charge of shot" at each corner "so as to prevent it flapping in the breeze." Experience led them to use string to tie the cloth down so there would not be "any terrifying flick of the cloth in the wind."

To photograph a bird's nest in a tall hedge or bush, the Kearton brothers simply mounted their tripod on improvised stilts cut from anything suitable growing locally, the camera being focussed by

Cherry, who stood on Richard's shoulders. Such animals as rabbits, hedgehogs and voles required a well-hidden camera plus considerable patience on the part of the operator. The camera was concealed. The operator, complete with binoculars, was at the other end of the pneumatic tube. When whatever-it-was came into the field of focus, the air-ball was squeezed and the shutter released. The technique of photographing at a distance with air-ball and pneumatic tube was used to photograph birds feeding their young at the nest. Winter shots of birds attracted to the garden by the food left for them were obtained with all but the camera lens covered by a white tablecloth. Cherry, who had considerable patience, waited a whole day to photograph a vole. Insect photography was most difficult and half a day elapsed before he successfully photographed a dragonfly on a stem of grass.

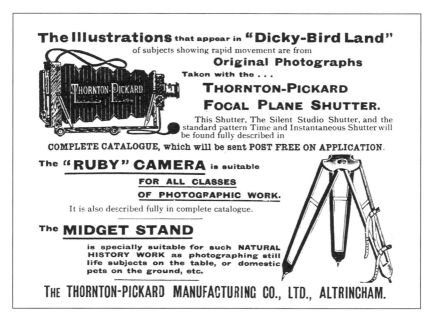

# Keeping Out of Sight

IT WAS Richard's idea to wear a coat of a mossy-green to tone with grass and bushes. Cherry wrily observed that at best it allayed the suspicions of birds and discouraged them from taking flight. What they most wanted was to photograph birds in their natural state. They must have a hiding place they could move to close quarters. They experimented with the hollow stub of an ash tree that Cherry drew over his head when standing in thick cover. "We soon found it was necessary to cover our whole bodies and also the camera." Artificial tree-trunks and imitation rocks could only be used in suitable country.

What would appear natural in the fields or alongside hedges? Rubbish heaps and imitation animals, of course! The rubbish heap idea began with a tent-like structure on which they piled sticks and dirt for naturalness. Cherry recalled: "I would squat down on the ground and then Richard would cover me with the framed canvas on to which he would pile all the rubbish he could find." It deceived "a pair of rustic lovers" who arrived "with arms around each other's waist and elected to sit in the pleasant shade of the heap; they billed and cooed just like the occupants of the nest I was trying to photograph."

Inspired by the story of how the Ancient Greeks had entered Troy surreptitiously in a Wooden Horse, they consulted Rowland Ward, the famous "animal-stuffer" of Piccadilly, and secured an artificial bullock, a cured skin was stretched over a light deal frame. "In the breast of the ox we had a small platform, upon which the camera, minus the tripod of course, stood propped into any desired angle by means of wooden wedges. The lens looked through one hole in the hide and the photographer watched his field of focus through another." Although awkward to carry about and difficult to use in breezy weather, unless its legs were tied to pegs driven into the ground, it deceived "birds of every kind" which "never appeared to notice that it stood upon six instead of four legs". They confidently approached a drinking place or nest by which the "stolid-looking creature" stood.

There were snags. The hide was back-aching to the operator and stuffy in hot weather. On the first outing, Cherry's legs descended through its stomach into a clump of weeds. "My brother left me and there I remained, crouching over the camera and ready to take photographs through a small hole in the animal's chest. I suffered considerably from cramp, but all would have been well but for the springing up of a gale which overturned the bullock and left me on my back inside the 'animal' in a small declivity, with my legs pointing at the sky." He remained in that uncomfortable position for an hour until Richard returned to relieve him.

The bullock was deployed at sites in Southern England. Soon the Keartons had a north-country variant, a stuffed sheep, in a recumbent position, the camera concealed within the body and a hole in the chest left "for the lens to look through". The focal plane shutter was worked from a distance by means of pneumatic tube. "Meadow pipits, wheatears and sandpipers were deceived by it, although the sudden discovery of the huge black eye staring straight at her nest from the breast of the sheep scared the last-named bird rather badly at first."

The modern hide – a small tent with a light frame and hessian or canvas cover – developed from experience with an imitation tree trunk for woodland and hedgerow and an artificial rubbish-heap to be used in open country. The "tree-trunk" consisted of three pieces of bamboo, each seven feet long, split down the centre and lashed to three small wooden hoops. This light structure was covered with American cloth, painted to resemble bark. Richard's wife painted the whole to represent a storm-snapped trunk and even added dabs of white to give the impression that birds had perched on it. Cherry glued on to it small pieces of moss and lichen. Richard added a final touch – sprays of ivy, "which we stripped from the trunks of trees as nearly in the same position as that in which they grew, so as to make the whole thing realistic."

Cherry, after a spell in the hide, signalled to his brother either by whistle or by thrusting the corner of a white handkerchief out of the back. All the fuss about making it look natural proved to be unnecessary. A simple frame covered with hessian or durable cloth would suffice. It was deduced that birds cannot count. If the two brothers walked to the hide and Richard walked away, the bird was soon back at the nest. Cherry photographed it with the lens of the camera protruding from a hole in front.

On windswept mountain tops, the hide used by the brothers was of the "rubbish-heap" variety set above a hip-deep pit excavated in peat or other workable material. The heap was adorned with heather. On rocky shores, they made a small stone hide, of horse-shoe shape, entered from behind. Any chinks in the "stone house" were covered up with turf so that the photographer was not visible. A variant on moorland was the "sod house". Richard photographed dippers, ring ouzels and curlews in Westmorland using an artificial rock made by a taxidermist friend who had premises in Croydon. The "rock" consisted of five separate pieces attachable to each other using hooks.

With such a wary bird as a curlew, he already adjudged that he must set down his hide at a distance and move it closer to the nest on successive days so as not to arouse the bird's suspicion.

Outdoors, when there was daylight, Cherry faced the problem of changing plates in his one and only "slide". He put the box of plates on the ground and covered them with his coat, the edges of which he fastened down with earth and stones. Then, on his knees, he slipped his hands down the sleeves of the coat into the lightproof recess and achieved the transfer of slide from box to slide. On a visit to his native Swaledale, he made the mistake of seeking the darkness of a disused lead mine. In the gloom, he missed his footing, fell into a hole, ruined his plates, a suit of clothes – and his temper. The answer to the problem proved to be a modification of the coat idea, with two lightproof sleeves leading into a lightproof bag.

In their field photography, the brothers were smartly dressed in tweedy clothes and wore cloth caps as a further mark of respectability. Climbing irons were available for ascending tall trees but Cherry, an adroit climber, rarely had use for them. Manilla hemp went into the ropes they had made for cliff work. Each rope was two hundred feet long. A revolver was available for what Richard described fulsomely as "the prosaic and harmless purpose of making a loud report at the top of any cliff in the face of which there is reason for believing some bird's nest, which we desire to photograph, is situated, so that by frightening its owner off we may locate the exact spot at which to make a descent." At a cliff-top, a crowbar was driven into the ground, "sloping slightly out of the vertical in a backward direction" and the rope tied to it. Another rope was used for guiding the climber. Cherry, walking backwards, would commence the descent of a cliff some seventy feet high, the bulky camera and tripod being lashed to his back.

Carrion crows seemed to prefer to nest near the top of a high isolated tree, the nest being a deep cup within which the eggs did not easily become chilled and from which they were unlikely to roll in windy conditions. The Keartons tackled a crow nest in March, 1896, checking on the progress of egg-laying by shinning part way up the tree with "our bit of looking-glass on the end of a rod". They then borrowed a twenty-foot ladder from a farmer, lashed almost vertically to branches at a considerable height above the ground and secured to it the legs of the tripod. When changing slides, Cherry held on to a rung of the ladder with his teeth, thus leaving his hands free.

The brothers photographed swallows on a telephone wire from a long ladder that had been reared against one of the interior walls of a high barn, the camera being lined up with a ventilator. "At the foot of the ladder, a chained bull was praying all the while in a deep bass voice that some unlucky slip might deliver the photographer and his bit of mahogany and brass over to his untender mercies."

# Adventures in Wild Places

IN HIS autobiography, entitled *A Naturalist's Pilgrimage*, Richard Kearton wrote: "We worked hard and honesty, sparing no pains, danger or expense in procuring what we considered interesting or instructive. For nights together we slept in empty houses and old ruins, descended beetling cliffs, swam to isolated rocks, waded rivers and bogs and climbed lofty trees. We lay in wet heather for hours at a stretch, tramped many weary miles in the dark and spent nights in the open air on lonely islands and solitary moors. On other occasions we endured the pangs of hunger and thirst and the torturing sting of insects, waited for days and days together for a single picture and were nearly drowned, both figuratively and literally. Yet such is the fascination of our subject that we endured all these and other inconveniences with the utmost cheerfulness."

They recounted their adventures in wild places in a well-illustrated book, *With Nature and a Camera*, telling of glorious days spent on the Farne Isles, Bass Rock, Ailsa Craig, the Inner and Outer Hebrides, St Kilda and the Saltee islands, off the south coast of Ireland. In their photographic work, they exhibited enterprise and tenacity. Richard considered that "the great secret of all field work is the power to keep absolutely still for a prolonged period of time." Cherry had this quality in abundant. He spent six days in patient waiting and watching for pictures of a kingfisher.

Otherwise, these two naturalists were in a hurry. In 1893, having visited Mull, in western Scotland, to take photographs at the eyrie of eagles, they sailed back to Oban and made their way down the coast to Girvan. At three o'clock in the morning, having hired a ferryman, they voyaged to Ailsa Craig, which loomed sheer out of the Clyde and was the breeding place of gannets. By breakfast-time, the brothers had reached the lighthouse and were seeking vantage points from which to photograph the huge seabirds.

When Cherry was satisfied, having found a flat slab of rock near the cliff-edge, he was horrified when the screw connecting camera to tripod became detached and was irretrievably lost over the cliff. His panic was momentary. He found a handy substitute in the moulted quill of a gannet. Cherry, having set up his camera, covered his head with the black cloth that shaded the focussing screen. He then had a sinking feeling. The rock on which he stood was slipping over the cliff edge. He clutched his camera, rolled sideways and "a second later the whole slab of rock plunged over the edge to fall hundreds of feet into the sea." Recovering his composure, Cherry found another site for his camera and photographed the gannets.

They visited Ailsa Craig in June, 1895, with one of the two brothers who rented the huge rock and who lived there. As they reached the rim of a cliff with a view of gannets nesting, the tenant said: "Mr Keeaarton, I have a verra perteeklar request to make… If you take my photograph, for goodness sake dinna promise to send me one; then it may come." Many visitors, including ministers of religion, who photographed him had promised to send him a copy, "but never one has reached me."

Scotland was a revelation to the brothers. Here, wrote Cherry, was wild country with rocky mountains, magnificent cliffs and wild seas. They were tenanted by peregrine falcons, gannets, eagles and a hundred other birds, "the very sight of which was beautiful and thrilling." Cherry could not expect Cassells to grant him several months' absence each year so he might continue his photographic record of Scottish wildlife. His immediate boss implied that he could not serve two masters. Deciding to take him at his word, Cherry left Fleet Street and entrusted his fate to his cameras.

In the early spring of 1894, he was back on Mull, re-visiting the eyrie of the eagles in the company of one of the gamekeepers of the

Duke of Argyll. On a subsequent visit, by himself, he was overtaken by a blizzard as he made his way down the mountain side. Cherry slipped, injured himself and damaged his camera to such an extent he had to take it to a chemist in Oban to be repaired. By the time both man and camera had been patched up, the chance of photographing the eaglets was passed so he visited other islands. On Acknakarry, Cherry spent the best part of three days in the loch, with the water often up to his chest, his camera focussed on the nest of the last pair of ospreys in Britain.

Cherry had the down-to-earth manner of the Yorkshire dalesman. He was fascinated by the ordinary Scottish folk. In the late spring of 1895, on a steamer out of Oban, plying among the Western Isles, he saw tourists, missionaries, Highland servants of both sexes on their way to or from engagements, commercial travellers, pedlars and migrants. "One hearty old Highland woman and her buxom daughter were moving to the bleak and lonely Isle of Rum with their few sticks of household furniture, a cow, yearling calf and half a dozen domestic fowls."

Noting as the voyage proceeded, that the cow's "bag" was distended with milk, Cherry offered to draw off the milk. This amused the old lady, to whom he appeared to be a visiting Cockney. Yet she assented. Richard borrowed a bucket from the chief steward and sat down to milk the animal. "I milked the flood of thin milk away into the bucket and, calling for a drinking glass, drew the rich remainder for a Highland railway manager, a missionary, my brother and myself. This piece of practical sagacity, proving that I knew the cow's richest milk is always given last, raised a red-headed Highlander's opinion of me considerably."

# Island-going with a Camera

WHEN RICHARD was having his main holiday from work, both brothers visited the rocky peripheral areas of Britain, such as Hermaness, on the isle of Unst, in Shetland. Here they were harried by bonxies [great skuas]. Cherry photographed the "watcher" as they swooped near his be-capped head. The watcher had been appointed and was paid by Laurence Edmondston, the landowner. Richard noted that the skua "generally appeared to make her terrific downward rushes from an altitude of about two hundred feet and a distance of seventy or eight yards. When she got close up to her enemy she dropped both feet and struck him on the back of his head as she passed over."

He examined a nest, in which one chick had hatched. The infuriated birds dived and repeatedly knocked off his cap. The blows "stung very sharply". Cherry, photographing with the camera set at a speed of "one-six-hundredth part of a second", portrayed the watcher's cap in the act of falling. The bird was travelling so fast it "got out of the plate altogether, with the exception of the tip of one wing." The brothers came within viewing distance of Muckle Flugga, "which marks the most northern point of the British Isles, and rather befittingly forms the tailpiece to this chapter."

Scotland remained a strong favourite with Richard and Cherry. On North Uist, in the Hebrides, every piece of cultivated land on the west side of the island seemed to be tenanted by the corncrake or landrail. Richard searched long and hard for a nest. Three pairs of birds were turned out of one field but no nest was located. Three or four more birds were flushed in the next field, with negative result. An elusive nest, with six eggs, was found on returning to the first field during the afternoon. They visited the nest to observe the progress of egg-laying and when eight eggs out of the full clutch of ten were present, a photograph was taken.

North Uist had also yielded a glimpse of half a dozen pairs of red-throated divers and one of the black-throated species. With the help of a gamekeeper, gillie and the factor's clerk, a heavy old fishing boat was dragged from the edge of a sea-loch over a rough, hilly stretch of moorland to a freshwater loch whereon divers were to be found, along with geese and gulls. The eggs had been laid in a sparse nest on an islet.

In the book *With Nature and a Camera* are details of a visit in 1896 to the Farnes, a scattering of rocky islands a mile or two off the Northumbrian coast. It was July, rather late in the seabird nesting programme. An association for the protection of seabirds employed several wardens, among them Robert Darling, the nephew of the immortal Grace Darling. They stayed three days and three nights with him in the ruins of St Cuthbert's Tower, sleeping in hammocks suspended from their climbing ropes, which were stretched across a haunted room.

Richard had the good fortune to be aroused by the tapping of a ghost at first light and promptly turned out to investigate. He found nothing for his brother's camera and magnesium ribbon except a huge piece of old oak pannelling, from which the sound emanated, possibly through some atmospheric change.

The brothers landed on the Megstones where there was a colony of breeding cormorants. One nest contained three fresh eggs but other nests held gawky young birds. "The sun was hot and the air almost still. Directly we set foot on the rock our nostrils were assailed by the foulest imaginable stench, arising from pieces of fish in all stages of decomposition, dead young birds trampled to incredible flatness and streams of liquid guano, which trickled down the sides of the crag and stood in festering pools in every crevice and declivity."

Most of the adult birds flew off; the young that could made an effort to escape over the slimy rock. An old female remained with the young on the nest, enabling Cherry carefully to stalk to within a few feet of her, when he took several photographic studies. On another island, they visited a huge ternery. Three species of tern – Sandwich, Arctic and common – were present. They used a young Sandwich tern in photographs that revealed the protective value of its coloration, first posing it on sand and then on a black cloth. (Elsewhere, they used the same ploy with a ringed plover chick). They had the good fortune to see and hear a roseate tern, its note being counted as similar in harshness to that of the corncrake. They gave up looking for the nest when the adult birds lost themselves in "the ever-changing, swooping, swirling throng of white-winged creatures."

A confiding eider duck remained on its down-lagged nest. An eider that nested at the foot of St Cuthbert's tower on the Inner Farne was absent for the first time for many years and the watchers concluded it had been shot during the winter. Richard wrote of the hardiness of eider ducklings that will "dash into a boiling sea from almost any height a day or two after they have made their advent into the world." The brothers sailed to the Bass Rock, courtesy of its owner, Colin Mackenzie of Canty Bay Hotel, who "owns every facility for conveying visitors in almost any sort of weather." Cherry did his usual display of confident cliffside stalking, his camera before him, high above the restless waves.

# Kearton Brothers

Richard Kearton (right) as he posed for a publicity photograph when his autobiography was published in 1926.

Cherry Kearton (left) as he was at the time of the Great War. He "shot" the first movie-film of that conflict and then served in East Africa. *(Courtesy of M Bentham).*

*Top:* Birthplace of the Kearton brothers at Thwaite, in Swaledale. *Bottom:* Muker School, where the brothers were educated. *(Courtesy of M Bentham).*

*Above:* Ellen Rose, the wife of Richard Kearton, had been an artist. *Below:* Grace, their daughter, who was a considerable help with photography.

Richard Kearton as a young man. He had been a cripple since boyhood.

*Right*: Sidney Galpin, son of the founder of the publishing company of Cassell, who offered Richard a job with the firm.

*Left*: One of the Kearton brothers' "hiding-tents" used for bird photography, before it was adorned with foliage. Inside are the photographer and camera on a tripod. *(From "Adventures with Animals and Men")*.

*Above:* Cherry, standing in water, focusses his camera on the nest of ospreys.

*Left:* Cherry dangles from a manilla rope while photographing seabirds. *(From "With Nature and a Camera").*

*Above:* A young kestrel, one of the subjects in a set of stereo pictures that were sold in about 1900 for 2s.6d.

The St Kilda mail-boat, from a photograph taken by the Kearton brothers when they sailed to the remote archipelago towards the end of the nineteenth century. *(From "With Nature and a Camera")*.

*Above:* Cherry on Penguin Island.
*Below, left:* Theodore Roosevelt. *Right:* Ada, wife of Cherry.

Cherry in Spencer's airship over London in 1908. He took the first movie-pictures of the city from the air. *Right:* Memorial plaque to Richard at Muker school.

THIS TABLET WAS ERECTED BY PUBLIC SUBSCRIPTION IN MEMORY OF RICHARD KEARTON F.Z.S. NATURALIST, AUTHOR AND LECTURER BORN 2ND JAN. 1862 DIED 8TH FEB. 1928 HE WAS EDUCATED AT THIS SCHOOL

# Wild Waters and St Kilda

IN THE summer of 1896, they visited a cluster of volcanic islands "at the edge of the world", on what Richard was to describe as "the greatest of our adventures". They were on specks of volcanic rock in the Atlantic nearly fifty miles off the west coast of the Outer Hebrides. To the brothers, St Kilda was "the paradise of British ornithologists". They were making arrangements for a visit as early as Christmas, 1895, and would accompany John Mackenzie, jnr., on his annual visit as factor.

They voyaged from Glasgow in the *Dunara Castle* on June 11, having received a telegram from Harvie-Brown, "the veteran naturalist of the North". Their considerable luggage including tinned provisions for themselves "and a quantity of sweets and tobacco for the natives." On the following days, the little steamer stopped at various Hebridean islands to discharge cargo. Early on the morning of June 13 they reached "weird and lonely" Obbe, which was their last calling place before the steamer braved the Atlantic waves.

The captain held out little hope of landing on Hirta if the stiff breeze from the south-east continued for it would make Village Bay untenable. Somewhat more optimistic was the official pilot, "a wrinkle-visaged, weather-beaten old man" who boarded the vessel at Obbe and was hopeful of an early change in the weather. Towards noon, the vessel was beyond the low, seal-haunted islands known as the Heiskers. A drizzling rain enfolded it as it rolled and pitched with accompanying porpoises and plunging gannets. Mackenzie pointed out a fulmar petrel, which then had a restricted range on the British coastline. Puffins, guillemots and razorbills were, encouragingly, on the same course as the steamer. Their first sight of St Kilda was sublime. "In front of us loomed the gigantic rock, with its summit buried in white mists and its base surrounded by a fringe of foam left by the broken billows."

Happily, after the turmoil of wind and waves in the open sea, they found Village Bay almost as smooth as the proverbial millpond. Richard wrote: "The St Kildans had no knowledge of the date of our coming and the dogs, numbering between thirty and forty, were the first to discover our presence in the bay." They tore pell-mell to the water's edge, barking furiously. The captain operated the steam whistle. The alarmed sheep on the hillside beyond the village scampered away. No one appeared. Another loud blast was sounded. A small boy ran down to the shore and gazed at the boat. Richard presumed that, taken by surprise, the populace was taking a little time to wash and tidied themselves before meeting the new arrivals.

When the brothers got ashore, they found that most of the women and children were awaiting them with handkerchiefs full of birds' eggs, mainly guillemots and razorbills, which were sold to passengers and crew of the steamer at a penny each. Apart from the joyous songs of the St Kilda wrens, the village was strangely quiet. Richard, Cherry and their friend John Young took over a cottage after sweeping up plaster that had fallen from the walls and lighting a fire in a grateless hearth. Cherry, in prowling around, looking for somewhere he might adapt as a darkroom, kept falling through rotten floorboards. The brothers slung their hammocks in two upper rooms. John Young, being somewhat rotund in form, who was in the next apartment, fell out of his hammock and other sleeping arrangements were made for him.

The Keartons, having been reared in a remote part of the Yorkshire Dales, had no difficulty in communicating with the St Kildans. They went to church, studied the local people and their customs, photographed the "peculiar little brown sheep", and posed the foot of the author alongside that of a St Kildan, to indicate the abnormal size of the latter's ankle joint. They met big Finlay MacQueen, who was already legendary, and then set to work to record the birds and fowlers of the islets. The men descended sheer cliffs on ropes to collect birds, eggs or young, to the St Kildans a vital natural resource to be eaten fresh or preserved.

Richard also rid them of at least one pest – a hooded crow. Having placed the entrails of a fish he had caught on the roof of a cleit, he spent a night in a neighbouring cleit with a gun at the ready. He was hoping for ravens but after a long and weary night of waiting and watching he settled for "one hooded crow less to trouble the natives of Hirta by stealing the eggs and young of their precious birds." Puffins were plucked, split open like kippers, cured and hung up to dry on strings stretched across the cottages "and whenever a native feels hungry he simply pulls one down from the line, flings it on the fire to grill and forthwith has his lunch without the aid of knife, fork, plate or napkin."

The brothers, together with Mackenzie, Young and the minister were accommodated in a small boat that crossed a short stretch of water to visit what they called the Doon and what is now known simply as Dun. Here the two Finlays, MacQueen and Gillies, demonstrated their skill with a fowling rod. Cherry worked his way to the edge of a cliff and positioned his camera to view several fulmars that were sitting on a ledge. He waited for the fowlers to descend. Finlay Gillies tied a rope round the body of MacQueen, who stealthily crept down, rod in hand, until he came within reach of the unsuspecting birds, dangling the noose just in front of the head of one of them. "By a dextrous twist of the wrist, the fatal circle of horse-hair and gannet quills fell round the neck of the fulmar, which instantly spread its wings and sprang forward, only to tighten the noose, and by its fluttering frighten all its companions away."

On another day, in another place, Richard lay on a spur of rock watching his brother make a precarious descent, with camera, to where fulmars were sitting. He saw a fulmar squirt a quantity of amber-coloured oil at Cherry. "It travelled three or four feet, describing a kind of half-circle and falling short of the mark." They came to recognise the preliminaries to such a squirt – the movement of the head and neck rapidly up and down as if trying to remove some obstacle from its throat.

The St Kildans needed an immense stock of fulmars. The oil was collected for their lamps. Fulmar feathers were mixed with those of other birds and sold to the government for stuffing soldiers' pillows. The oil gave off such a strong odour that everything smelled of it. Though fumigated before being used, feathers regained the smell in about three years and had to be roasted once again before a soldier would rest his sleeping head on them.

Richard and Cherry also paid much attention to the smallest of the birds – the St Kilda wren, which was claimed to differ in some respects from the mainland wren. Richard obtained an adult male and found that from the point of its bill to the tip of its tail it measured four and a-quarter inches. (A specimen of the same sex in southern England was four inches long). Richard concluded that the beak, legs, toes and claws of the St Kilda bird are "a trifle stronger and lighter in colour and the plumage generally paler and more distinctly marked. This is especially noticeable on the back, which is barred transversely with greyish and dark brown, where the mainland bird is reddish brown with indistinct bars of a darker hue."

Richard observed that the St Kildan wren rarely if ever cocked its tail at that acute angle so characteristic of the common wren. "Its song is about the same duration as that of the mainland bird, viz. from five to six seconds; is louder, less metallic and much oftener uttered on the wing. I sometimes heard it within a few inches of my ear whilst standing perfectly still in a cleit... I never once heard the familiar jarring note of alarm or anger so common in other parts of the British Isles."

Having captured a young wren during a visit to the island of Soay, Richard held it while Cherry fixed up his camera and focussed on the corner of a crag. "When he had got his plate in and all ready, I quietly placed the bird upon the crag and kept my hands over the little creature until he was composed; then counting one, two, for my brother's signal, I swiftly withdrew. The pneumatic tube was instantly pressed and a photograph taken." To photograph a nest over the door-lintel inside a cleit, Cherry fixed a looking-glass at such an angle inside the cleit that it reflected light back to the nest. Richard then went outside and with another mirror "threw the sun's rays upon the looking-glass inside." A long exposure and several intermittent gleams of sunshine produced an acceptable photograph.

When the sea was calm, they visited the island of Boreray, with Finlay MacQueen in the boat's company, voyaging near Stac Lee, "a gigantic pillar of rock rising about three hundred feet out of the ocean" and clouded by swirling gannets. "As far as the eye could see small objects, the sea was covered… by a vast throng of puffins, guillemots and razorbills." Boreray was "sternly guarded by its dark bulwark of forbidding crags, from the topmost edges of which brilliant green slopes of great steepness ran upwards until they were lost in the trailing skirts of a luminous white cloud. With waves smacking their lips against smooth rock, which was festooned by weed, they had difficulty in landing from the boat.

Cherry devised a special technique for transferring the precious camera and photographic plates from boat to shore, tying the camera to the middle of a long rope, one end of which was thrown to a man ashore and hauled in by him, "whilst the part behind the apparatus is being paid out in such a way as to keep the whole taut, and thus prevent the camera from swinging or touching the rocks."

Richard was recommended by his brother to stay in the boat but, cripple though he was, he could not resist landing. They struggled up a steep cliff to where the island was covered by turf, into which a vast number of puffins had driven their nesting burrows. Richard wrote that "the clouds of birds that swept past us made a sound like a whirlwind whipping a great bed of dead rushes." They reached into burrows in which they supposed "fork-tailed petrels" were nesting. "I had not investigated more than two or three holes before I felt a particular stinging pain and precipitately withdrew my hand, streaming with blood. I had invaded the nest of a Tammy Norrie [puffin] by mistake."

Finlay MacQueen demonstrated how to catch puffins with a fowling-rod – a light deal pole about thirteen feet long, with a hazel twig between two and three feet in length lashed to the end. To this was securely fastened a running noose of horse-hair and gannet quills. With the noose stiffened, it might be slipped over the head of a bird with a dextrous turn of the wrist. "So successful are the St Kildans at this kind of sport that Angus Gillies once bagged to his own rod no less than six hundred and twenty puffins in a single day." Other members of the party appeared from a different quarter of the island, laden with fulmars and puffins. Richard was double-roped for safety as he was switched from the island to the "frail old boat, which a month or two later – according to a letter I had from Finlay MacQueen – went to splinters on the rocks during a gale."

The brothers made a hazardous landing and climb on the island of Soay [a Norse name relating to sheep] where they found "a prodigious flock of puffins." On the way to Soay, they landed in a cliffscape, where they came across a shag nest holding downy young and "a great number of razorbills' eggs lying about under boulders and ledges." Here and there was a newly-hatched young bird. Soay proved to be "the most awkward island to effect a landing upon which we had yet encountered."

Richard persuaded Finlay Gillies to lay a puffin snare on a jutting rock. The snare consisted of a "bit of rope, weighted at either end with a stone and crowded with about forty horse-hair nooses in the middle." An inquisitive puffin pecked at some of the nooses then unwisely put a foot in one of them. "In a little while, two more Tammy Norries became fast... Finlay Gillies stepped along the crag and, sitting down upon one of the stones securing the snare... had his portrait taken, along with that of the birds he had secured, in a position from which the slightest slip would have meant a headlong plunge of five hundred feet into the ocean below." Naturally, Cherry also made a separate photograph of the "puffin gin", stretched out to show the many nooses.

The brothers, with their equipment and valuable stack of photographic plates, left St Kilda on the *Hebridean*. The captain took her round by Stac Lee, near which some members of the crew ran out a small brass canon. "The tip of a red-hot poker applied to the touch-hole of the gun produced a deafening explosion which seemed to be instantly flung back at us by Stac Lee and then thundered and reverberated from crag to crag along the rocky sides of Boreray, sending a great white cloud of startled gannets into the air above us.

Cherry left the boat at Benbecula, intent on visiting Skye to stay with H A Macpherson, a naturalist friend. There was an alarming experience for Richard when the vessel, in mist, struck a sunken rock. Richard "dived below for my box of St Kilda negatives, which had been stowed away for safety in the grog cellar beneath the saloon deck, now thickly strewn with broken wine glasses that had been shaken from their place over the dining table... Luckily for us the sea was smooth and the tide rising. By shifting all the passengers and a quantity of the deck cargo aft, and going full-steam astern, after about twenty minutes of suspense we ground our way off the rock into deep water."

# Eggs and Egg-collecting

THE KEARTONS had sought bird nests since their first excursions into the dale-country. They were familiar with almost every bird that bred in Britain. In 1890, when Richard was living at Boreham Wood, Elstree, Herts., he wrote *Birds' Nests, Eggs and Egg-Collecting*. It was illustrated by colour plates. So successful did this become it was soon re-printed, then issued in an enlarged form in 1896. This book went through six re-prints between then and 1907. He included advice on forming a collection of bird eggs.

A collector must keep watch on the building operations of the bird whose egg was required. Only one specimen should be taken from a nest and the clutch should be left intact if there were grounds to suppose that incubation had begun. The drill and blow-pipe needed to prepare the egg for the collection were said to be available at any naturalist's shop. When the contents had been emptied, the egg should be washed out using clean water. The hole in the egg should be covered with a neat piece of gummed paper on which the name of the specimen may be written. A collector might have to buy or exchange through the medium of an advertisement eggs of species that did not nest in his or her area.

In later life, Richard was horror-struck by the effect egg-collecting was having, especially on rarer species of birds. In the book he titled *Our Rarer British Breeding Birds*, published nine years after the first appearance of his work on egg-collecting, he wrote: "When, in spite of all the protective legislation devised by the wisdom and experience of British statesmen and ornithologists, it is possible for one of our very rarest birds to be robbed of its eggs for ten years in unbroken succession, and when collectors boast that with a bottle of whisky and a kettle of hot water they can possess themselves of any specimen they desire, the present conditions of things is manifestly hopeless."

Eggs protected by law were still hunted by "children, young men and old men, maidens and white-haired dames". Some even waited for hours until the eggs had been laid. "The Wild Bird Protection laws are very like a beautiful padlock and chain, hanging useless on a widely-opened stable-door which it is nobody's business to lock." There were private individuals with an impulse to protect birds. He instanced the great skuas of Unst, eiders on the Farne Islands and the lesser tern [sic] at Wells, in Norfolk. Publicity in cases where wrong-doers came before the Courts simply drew attention to nesting places hitherto known only to a few.

He instanced the red-necked phalarope as one of the species most persecuted for the sake of its eggs. The last pair of phalaropes attempting to breed on the island of Unst, the most northerly in the Shetland group, had been shot by a local gunner a week before the Keartons arrived to photograph it. A collector had been found waist deep in a North Uist bog impudently blazing away with a double-barrelled gun "and not a single phalarope has ever been seen there since." In another of the isles of the west, "a despicable individual took advantage of the poor bird's absurd tameness and tried his best to extirpate it with a catapult."

As Richard approached this nesting place, "I was besieged by a number of boys and girls who asked me whether I wanted to buy phalaropes' eggs. One of the latter told me rather boastfully that she had sold a clutch for one shilling and tenpence. The odd twopence off the round sum plainly indicated to me the business acumen of the pedlar. During my stay I saw members of both sexes and all ages, from lisping little toddlers to grey-headed old men and women, systematically searching the environs of the marsh for eggs, and it is surprising that any birds should be left to come back summer after summer to attempt the almost hopeless task of perpetuating their species."

They sought the nest of a pair of kites in a remote part of Wales where they were said to be protected. One pair owed "their discovery and ruin" to the fact that their ancient stronghold happened to have been the hiding-place of some Elizabethan outlaw, "at whose shrine numbers of admirers worship every year." The Keartons visited the place but "found nothing except grounds for suspicion that they had already been robbed."

Richard and Cherry had to be content to photograph an old nest in a high tree. The kites were repairing it. The brothers had tried to save a kite nest in Wales by appealing in *The Field* for money to defray expenses. Alas, the eggs were stolen. Dutifully, the brothers returned the money to the subscribers – and stood any expense out of their own pockets. Local farmers were annoyed about the robbery, having discovered the monetary value of kite eggs. "They felt they had been done out of something!"

Even in the Keartons' home territory on the fells where Yorkshire was on nodding terms with Westmorland, decreases in bird life were noted. Sometimes, as with the golden plover, the reason was obscure. They photographed the nest of a pair of golden plover not far from Nine Standards Rigg, which overlooks Kirkby Stephen. "The bird has decreased, from some cause or other, during the last fifteen years… My brother and I found only two nests during a whole day's search in the spring of 1897, although we discovered a good number of dunlin nests."

# Family Matters

THE MOTHER of Richard and Cherry, who eventually lived at Nateby, near Kirkby Stephen, died in January, 1895. Richard had promised her that she would be interred in the same plot in Muker churchyard where her husband had been buried. On the funeral day, a blizzard had dramatically changed the contours on the road that wended its way for sixteen miles through wild country between Mallerstang and Swaledale. Richard employed a gang of men to cut through the drifts. The coffin reposed on a horse-drawn sled and was followed by mourners who were mounted on ponies. After the burial, the party made its slow way back to Nateby, arriving about midnight.

In 1887, Richard had been married to Ellen Rose Cowdry and they set up house at Caterham in Surrey, subsequently having a family of three sons and two daughters, one of whom, Grace, was to become his secretary. Grace, born on 9 February, 1892, grew up to become a first-rate naturalist and to have the practical skills needed to assist her father. She organised his appointments and accompanied him on natural history expeditions. And she assisted Uncle Cherry in the development of his photographs. Cherry was married to Mary Coates in 1900; they had two children – Cherry Edward and Morella.

Richard, who at Cassells had worked his way up to publicity manager, suffered a bad attack of influenza in the spring of 1898. His condition was neglected. His health deteriorated. And he was advised to get out of London. He was also compelled to leave the daily job he loved. He moved to Caterham and in the woods and fields near his home he accomplished many more natural history studies, to be joined by Cherry when something special was detected, such as when the nest of kingfishers was found.

One winter, when the streams in Surrey were swollen and muddy, the kingfisher visited a friend's garden in which there was a goldfish pond. The bird sat on an ash sapling beside the pond or upon the trailing boughs of a tree overhanging the other side. Cherry was interested. A resourceful friend cut a round hole in the side of a large wooden box. This was placed on a gravel-path near the ash sapling, being moved closer each day so the kingfisher would not be upset.

An old door was used to mask the photographer as he approached. The gravelly path was overlaid with sacks to deaden the sound of his boots. Cherry placed his camera in the box, focussed it on the bird's favourite twig through the hole, ran out pneumatic tubing from the camera to a point behind the old door – and kept watch from the sitting room of the house. Patience had its reward. The kingfisher was photographed in close-up.

Grace was fond of recalling when she helped to photograph prim-roses at Caterham at midnight, to mark the start of the twentieth century. She pressed the bulb on the cable that released the shutter while Uncle Cherry set light to a magnesium ribbon for the flashlight exposure.

Grace met her husband, Howard Bentham, through an interest in birds. Richard Kearton and Howard collaborated in the production of *The Pocket Book of British Birds*, which was subtitled "the who's who of the bird world."

# Cherry and the Nightingale

IMAGINE A tall figure with a huge box on his chest, kept in position by straps passing round the back of his neck, exactly like an organ-grinder, and carrying a large trumpet. The figure was Cherry Kearton, anxious to record on wax cylinder the song of the nightingale. He was not successful but never forgot the stresses of "stalking through the silent woods weighed down with all that apparatus", terrified lest he should "tread on the tiniest twig, or brush against hanging branches, for fear of disturbing the precious songster."

Cherry's fascination with recording bird-song could be dated from about the year 1900, when he was living in Surrey. He invested about £50 in an Edison phonograph that worked with big wax cylinders and had a special Edison Bell recorder and repeater. He had been intending to make "this great purchase" to enable him to record the songs of the birds he spent so many hours photographing. The state of the art of recording was not good enough – more precisely, quiet enough – for the purpose he had in mind.

His first subject was a thrush singing on a bush on a common near Kenley. He had noticed that about 6 a.m. it perched there and sang for almost an hour. "Accordingly I hollowed out some of the bush and fixed my heavy phonograph on a strong tripod and placed it in position, arranging the trumpet within a couple of feet of the bird's favourite position." It was a particular cold morning. He hid and waited. When the bird arrived, his hand shook with excitement as he moved the level to start the recorder. Suddenly, there was a loud crack, "just like ice breaking in a hard frost", and the bird's song abruptly ended. The cold air had contracted the wax on the metal cylinder and it broke into two pieces. "There I had to wait, cramped and cold, until the bird departed, after which I hurried away, very depressed."

That evening, Cherry called on Mr Hough, at Edison's, for some advice. No solution was given to the problem on how to safegard the instrument against extreme climatic conditions. Cherry's answer was to make a cover for the recorder. His patience was rewarded when he heard the bird singing within a few feet of his head. Once again he moved the starting-lever. The recorder began to emit a faint hissing sound as it cut through the wax. It had recorded only a few notes when the bird stopped singing, put off it seemed by the sound of the recorder cutting the wax. He ran through the whole cylinder, hoping to accustom the bird to the sound. The experiment was a failure.

He used the cover of night to record a nightingale and had a similar experience. "Night after night I crept to within a few feet of the bird as it sang in the strange stillness." At that time, he was commuting daily by train into the City. After telling a fellow passenger about his experience, his friend made what to him was a gratifying remark: "Kearton – you'll always be twenty-five years before your time."

# Into the Air

CHERRY had so often photographed birds in flight, he took the first opportunity to see the world from their angle. In May, 1908, when the Spencer brothers decided to fly their airship – the first in Britain – over London and to circle round St Paul's Cathedral, Cherry determined to go with them. He hoped to expose what he believed would be the first cine-film to be taken from the air. When he got in touch with Charles Urban, a pioneer of the film industry, who projected topical films at the *Alhambra*, it was arranged that when the film was taken it should be dropped on the roof of Urban's new studios in Wardour Street.

The flight, on 4 May, commenced from a field beside some gasworks, just outside London. The airship looked strange but awesome – a seventy-foot long gasbag, pointed at each end, with a frail-looking arrangement of bamboo rods suspended from netting. Cherry was to write: "The airship was certainly not a Zeppelin, but in those days, when one was accustomed only to pear-shaped balloons, it seemed an extraordinary sight. At the centre of the forty foot long framework was the basket which would hold three people. The usual sandbags were hung round the outside of the basket."

The propellor, made of gas-tubing, was situated in the bow with a canvas rudder protruding from the stern. The engine – "somewhat larger than a modern motor-cycle engine" – lay nearly half-way between basket and propeller. To attend it, one of the crew must walk along one of the lower bamboo poles of the framework, gaining further support by clasping the upper bar.

When the airship became airborne, it appeared to be intent on colliding with a large building. "But the ship answered the helm and we were rising rapidly, so that we cleared the roof with a few feet to spare. Then up we went and straight towards London." The Thames resembled a silver snake. The roofs of buildings formed tiny rectangular patterns. Fields were like a limitless chessboard and thin, pale, winding streaks were roads. At an elevation of between three and four thousand feet, the engine began to backfire and the pace of the propeller slackened. The airship heeled over, "canted on one side, seemed to think of turning round and then decided against it. At one second the nose pointed upwards, at the next it pointed downwards."

In next to no time, a thousand feet of height was lost. Spencer released some of the sandbags "and with extraordinary swiftness we rose – not climbing upwards and forwards, but simply rising straight like a balloon." They were now enveloped in clouds. From the engine came a series of explosions. There was a strong smell of gas. A big bang followed. They floated in silence. The engine stopped when the petrol pipe fractured. "By all the rules we ought to have gone up in a sheet of flame and then to have tumbled, charred and unrecognisable, to the earth. Why we didn't, I don't know."

Now floating at fourteen thousand feet, the crew felt uncomfortable. Cherry's nose was bleeding. "I felt the hammering of piston-rods in both my ears." He pulled himself together – and began taking some photographs. It was vital to lose weight. The sand had gone. Spencer pointed to the camera, implying that it should be tossed overboard, but it was lashed to the bamboo frame. Cherry brought it into play as the ground seemed to rise to meet them.

The framework of the airship hit the ground violently. "We were thrown off our feet and fell into a confusion of bamboo and tubing and pipes, with the gasbag all on top of us; but we scrambled out unhurt and suffering only from what the newspapers would now call 'bruises and shock'." The camera was undamaged. So was the film, which was being shown to Londoners on the following day – the first film of the Metropolis to be taken from the air.

Caterham Valley
Surrey
13/4/26

My Dear Frank,

"Pilgrimages" + "Pocket Book" herewith. Pray excuse delay, brought about by waiting to get my son-in-law's autograph in the latter book.

Things are going ahead here at a great rate. We have two Hedge Sparrows and a Blackbird sitting in gdn and Orchard a robin building in an old kettle, a Chaffinch building in a birch tree just outside our dining room, + tits and Wrens busy round nesting boxes. Jack found a Long T. Tits nest with eggs in yesterday + saw a lot of Sand Martins. Pear + apple trees in bloom.

Excellent reviews appearing in London Papers of my Life. Glad to say it is selling well in this neighbourhood.

With kind regards I remain
Always faithfully Yrs
R Kearton

A letter written by Richard Kearton to Frank Lowe,
a young Lancashire naturalist.

# Dales and Fells

ON THEIR visits to the Dales, the brothers made use of every minute in recording not only wildlife but some of the rural characters, including the grouse-poacher, once a thorn in the side of the gamekeeper but, by 1911, an almost vanished figure. Richard had known an old chap who, on a moonlit night, when there was snow on the ground, donned a white shirt and a pair of sheep-shearing drawers with which to creep up on a covey of roosting grouse and slay them with his old shotgun.

The brothers met and photographed a poacher who rented a small tract of heather-clad freehold land that was surrounded by some of the best grouse moors in the land. As soon as the shooting season began, he planted two thousand copper wire snares, which he called "hanks", in the sheep tracks along which the grouse loved to run and erected nets on his domain that intercepted birds in flight. This man had sometimes taken as many as fifteen brace of grouse out of his snares in a single morning. He obligingly allowed himself to be photographed in the act of re-setting one from which he had just obtained a bird which, at that time, might be seen protruding from his jacket pocket.

This activity was not illegal, for the man had a licence to kill game and was doing it on land to which he had legal access. The law insisted that he must take up all his snares on Saturday night. As Richard observed: "The Sabbath must not be broken by profane bits of wire hanging about like round O's among the heather. Our old friend was caught napping in this direction… and was fined for his wickedness."

The lessee of the surrounding moor took every opportunity of spoiling the old chap's sport. He tethered a brace of falcons to scare the grouse away from that bit of moor but they came within legal reach of his gun and perished. A number of flags set up all around mysteriously disappeared one dark night. A wooden hut that accommodated two watchers accidentally caught fire while the aforementioned watchers were imbibing at a farmhouse in the dale.

A shepherd directed the Kearton brothers to the nest of a pair of golden plover containing new-hatched chicks, their down flecked with gold. Richard dropped his cap over two chicks and then, with what he would call "picturesque rashness", made a sod house five feet away, using turves dug out by spade and a roof-frame made from the remnants of a sheepfold gate. He then removed his cap – and got successful photographs of a bird and the chicks.

Further afield, they spent days studying and photographing the osprey "at home on a lonely loch buried deep amongst the giant hills of Auld Scotia." As they rowed a boat close in to the islet where the bird was breeding, the female was seen "standing erect, like a feathered sentinel, at the very tip of the withered stump rising above her eyrie." She took flight "and throwing up her wings, allowed her body and legs to droop as if she had broken her back, the while uttering her peculiarly weak alarm note." When, much later, the male bird arrived, a fine large trout was clasped in its talons.

A study of an osprey at the nest was taken by Cherry, using one of his telephoto lenses. At the time the shutter was released, he had been waist-deep in the loch for two hours "in weather none too bright or warm."

The little grebe (or dabchick) that Cherry photographed had its nest near the middle of a wide Suffolk dyke. The brothers reached it using a long plank, for the wind was blowing hard and cold and the prospect of having to stand hip-deep in water, with a subsequent long journey to dry clothes, was distinctly unpleasant. Cherry and a local man shielded the reeds from the wind with a large travelling rug while Richard photographed the nest. He noted: "Once when an uncommonly strong gust of wind struck the rug and its holders, they had the narrowest escape possible of falling head-first off their plank into the water… My brother saved the situation by letting go his end of the rug and thus spilling the wind."

A ladder was used to reach the nesting hole of nuthatches in one of the lime and chestnut avenues of Torquay. A local friend, Charles Snell, reported the birds were present through the year. In winter, "some considerate bird-lovers" fed them with Barcelona nuts. The nuthatch nest was tucked out of sight and the Keartons had to be content to measure the plaster with which the birds had adroitly reduced the size of the hole to one that perfectly suited their small bodies. "The plaster was composed of the red earth of the country, small pebbles and road scrapings and was as hard as if a quantity of cement had been mixed with it." Richard examined a nuthatch nest in Sussex. He could see the bird sitting on the nest but was unable to dislodge her!

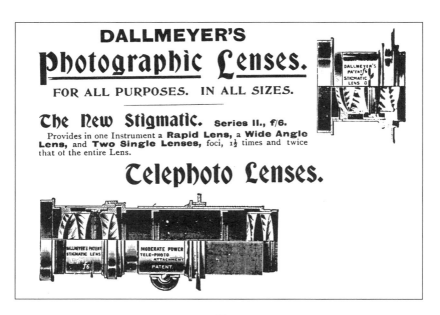

# Erin's Isle

IN THE halcyon years before the Great War, Richard returned to some of the haunts he had known in the pioneering days, when the photography had been left to Cherry. One fine May morning, he met his friends Richard Ussher, author of *Birds of Ireland*, and Richard Barrington, for a sail to the Saltee Islands, off the Wexford coast. Among a mass of photographic equipment owned by Richard were "natural colour plates and sundry ordinary ones."

The small boat was well provisioned and he was assured they would have a comfortable stay because a carpenter had been sent to reglaze the broken windows of an empty farmhouse and "there was plenty of old hay in the bedrooms for us to sleep upon." The workman had fitted a new brass catch to a window, which prevented the frame from closing by an inch or two. This did not matter. He had forgotten the sheets of new glass. Sundry holes in the window were plugged with wisps of hay.

The Saltees appeared to be alive with what used to be known as seafowl. Richard was to recall, in *Wonders of Wild Nature*, a book that appeared in 1915: "Kittiwakes dotted the cliffs like snowflakes... Everywhere, amongst rich carpets of bluebells and sorrel, great black-backed, lesser black-backed and herring gulls had their nests. On the bare honeycombed peat banks above the cliffs stood hundreds of puffins gazing at us in clownish curiosity. Shags were sitting on their eggs amongst rough boulders and cormorants already had well-grown young ones in their dirty, foul-smelling nests."

Richard stalked a cormorant with his movie-camera. He had reeled off about fifty feet of film when he realised that the old cormorant was standing as still as a statue. He got some animated pictures after he had tossed towards it a large piece of dry peat which "to my astonishment, and the cormorant's also, landed squarely on her back."

One morning, the visitors went looking for the eyrie of peregrine falcons in a "wee cove" when they saw a battle between two kittiwakes, the stronger bird driving the other down from the cliffs into the sea "and there deliberately holding its head under water until it was drowned and floated away upon the tide – a pathetic bundle of dishevelled lifeless feathers." On another day, they found the eyrie – "a mere hollow in the black-peat mould" – with two newly-hatched chicks and an egg. Richard resisted the temptation to photograph the young in case they became chilled and died.

The island was inhabited by rabbits and rats. "Our old boatman, who had farmed the island in days gone by, told me that he had often known rats to kill and devour rabbits... When hard-pressed, rats will hunt and kill domestic mice. They leave the skin behind turned inside out, very much in the way as skins of small leverets or young rabbits are left when devoured by a predatory cat."

Each evening, the little party sallied forth to listen for the Manx shearwaters. They were silent – or perhaps non-existent, having been banished by the hordes of hungry rats. On the day they were to depart, the weather improved and Richard "rushed out early with the whole battery of my apparatus. By dint of careful stalking I managed to come near enough to several individual herring gulls to enable me to expose a couple of natural colour plates and sundry ordinary ones upon the birds. I tried one or two great black-backed gulls, also lesser black-backs, but they were too shy and wary, so I ran off a couple of hundred feet of film with my kinematograph camera upon herring gulls alighting upon boulders of rocks near their nests, flying away again, and in other phases of their breeding activity."

To photograph cormorants on a detached rock at the Saltees, where they were staying with Ussher, Cherry swam for twenty or thirty yards with a rope round his neck. It was then possible to get the cameras to him on the rope and with only the legs of the tripod touching the water. On the first attempt at swimming, his legs became entangled in seaweed and a breaking wave hurled him against the rocks from which he had just started. He was badly bruised and cut. When he reached the cormorants' crag, blood was trickling down both legs.

He took his camera to the nest of a pair of choughs that lay on a small ledge in a cave. The necessary exposure was estimated at fifteen minutes. He and Ussher were cut off by the tide and, the ropes they had used to reach the cave now being out of reach, Cherry had to make a gruelling, skin-removing ascent of a crack in a cliff to where he could complete the climb and shift the ropes to where Ussher was about to be washed away.

# Off to Africa!

IN 1907, Richard favourably reviewed in a London newspaper a book that had been written by zestful, wildlife-loving Theodore (Teddy) Roosevelt, President of the United States. He received a letter of thanks from the author and they "drifted into a friendly correspondence upon matters of mutual interest." The upshot was an invitation to visit America to meet Roosevelt and deliver some lectures.

One Saturday, in March, 1908, Richard arrived in Washington. Sunday was spent  touring the city. On Monday he lunched with Roosevelt at the White House. The President, "seething with energy and bubbling over with high spirits", shook the visitor's hands and said he was dee-lighted to welcome him to the United States. After lunch, they were driven to a tract of virgin forest on the banks of the Creek River for a "bird hunt".

Richard saw, for the first time, chickadees, hairy woodpeckers and cardinal birds. The President, who had a boyish manner, a fast pace and limited time, was not one to sit down and contemplate his surroundings. He was "rushing up steep banks, tearing through tangled masses of undergrowth and floundering down slippery braes..." Richard, having only one suit with him in America, was saddened to find his trousers spattered with mud, which also clung to his boots. Consequently, when the trip was over, he asked the President to drop him some distance from the hotel where he was staying. He crept in unseen.

Another day, Roosevelt showed Richard an American kingfisher and wood duck at their nests. "He knew their respective haunts almost to the yard and, by careful stalking, secured me an excellent view of each bird. We were fortunate enough to watch the former... catching a fish." When Richard assumed the role of lecturer, he had the support of two lanternists as he showed his slides and movies.

In 1909, having photographed a goodly number of birds on the British List, Cherry Kearton, fired by the adventures of the great Victorian explorers, and knowing that Roosevelt was planning to visit East Africa, took his large cine-camera, which was hand-cranked, to the Dark Continent. With the President of the United States in Africa, the trip was bound to be well-publicised. There should be widespread interest in any films he shot.

Cherry, who had grown up in the shadow of Kisdon, the "island hill" in Swaledale, now beheld Mount Kilimanjaro, rising proud and majestic through the clouds above the dusty African plain. Never happy when cooped up indoors, he had quit his job with Cassells and had become the first freelance photographer of wildlife. His companion was an American naturalist, James L Clark, who was familiar with the safari concept.

Cherry's depiction of African wildlife, which was widespread and profuse in the early years of the nineteenth century, was through photographs and vivid anecdotal writing. He visited two areas where the Old Africa is still apparent, these being the Serengeti Plain and the Ngorongoro Crater. One remarkable film was made while following the route of Stanley, in the Congo. It yielded not only film but a chimp named Toto, the subject of one of his many books. On that first African journey, in 1909, he travelled by small cargo boat to Mombassa, thence by train to Nairobi. His first shock came at daybreak on the first morning after he boarded a train. Glancing out of the window at what he had imagined would be unrelieved jungle, he saw instead an enormous tract of open country dotted with bushes or small trees.

The view reminded him of home, except for the profusion of animals. Across the plain roamed large herds of zebra, hundreds strong, gazelle and buck. He was as yet too inexperienced to distinguish between the different varieties but into view came "several groups of giraffe, a rhino, then smaller creatures in the distance… the country, as I saw it that morning from the train, simply teemed with animal life."

The animals were even more numerous on the great Athi Plains, "which are seventy miles across and covered with grass with hardly a single bush or tree. Herds of zebra must have been at least a thousand strong, their stripes standing out against the dull greenish-brown of the landscape and thrilling me with their possibilities for picture-making." When he got down to work with his camera, "all that paradise seemed to fade like a mirage. Herds that would only stand and stare at the train would bound away in terror when I, alone, walked within two hundred yards of them."

Camping was not as joyful an experience as he had imagined. "I didn't lie and listen to birds: I sought desperately for sleep hour after hour in the night amid a hundred uncomfortable noises – the ghastly laugh of the hyena, the cry of the jackal, the puffing of a rhinoceros. And when at last sleep came, I would be roused almost at once – roused with a quaking start by the roar of a lion."

Cherry found that the type of hides that were successful in Britain hardly worked in Africa. He thought of adapting some of them, so that instead of using a dummy sheep he might have a dummy zebra. His hunting friends pointed out how easy it would be for them to shoot that zebra – with Cherry inside it. What would he propose to do if the "zebra" was stalked by a lion? Building a screen in order to photograph a herd of eland, he waited, then looked up to see his gaze being returned by a huge python, which he promptly shot.

He photographed the birds of Lake Naivasha and the hippos that inhabited the Tana River. For waterfowl, he had a long-legged chair built and laid on a platform built across two boats, from which he had it lowered into the water some fifty yards from the shore of his chosen lake. He fixed reeds around it, took his seat – with his feet just touching the water – and was closely boxed in with reeds by his boys, who then left him, with instructions not to return for four hours. He secured photographs of Egyptian geese, lily trotters, ibis, herons, storks and bitterns. Thankfully, the hippo that lived in the lake did not collide with his chair-hide.

He put his cine-camera to work on hippos, including about fourteen of the creatures that were "playing in the water, basking in the sunlight and occasionally diving but always re-appearing within easy range of my camera." Hippo and crocodile basked together. "There were water-tortoises nesting close to the crocodiles' jaws and birds waiting to pick parasites out of the crocodiles' teeth. I felt then that for all the trouble I had had during my first three months in Africa, I was amply repaid."

In lion country, and carrying rifles, Cherry and Clark were attended by two of the Masai armed with spears. A boy carried Cherry's camera. "The boy with the camera was leading – at least, he was leading at one minute and the next… he was away behind us, running for all he was worth. The Masai started running too; and so did Clark and I. We weren't sure what we were running from but we were in an open stretch of country with no possible protection from danger except a single tree forty yards away, and we all ran towards that. Then, as we stopped, panting, and turned, the danger was apparent: two great rhinos were charging straight at us."

Masai spears did not halt their progress; the American's gun jammed and Cherry fired when the rhino was so close the animal collapsed within inches of him. Cherry rose, looked for the other rhino in a cloud of dust, and then on impulse ran round the lee side of the tree, to collide shoulder to shoulder with the three-ton rhino. Cherry fell, bruised. The rhino departed at high speed, leaving the dead body of his mate.

In his book *Adventures with Animals and Men*, Cherry recounted his meeting with Theodore Roosevelt, the holidaymaking President of the United States, whose large party unaccountably lacked anyone with a movie camera. His son Kermit was the stills photographer.

Now, in Africa, the President wanted a break from photo-calls. As he left Nairobi on his way to Mount Kenya, Cherry was among those who saw him off. Roosevelt took Cherry's arm and they walked up and down the platform, waiting for the train. The President asked Cherry if there was anything he could do to help and was asked if he would allow Cherry to take "a few feet of film".

Roosevelt agreed and was subsequently photographed watching a big ingoma [native war dance] in which two thousand natives, wearing fantastic head-dresses and carrying spears and gaily-painted shields, formed shoulder to shoulder in a huge circle and danced. "All the while, they chanted dirges and jangled bells that were tied to their knees, and over all there came the steady, monotonous beating of the drums."

Then two of them went mad and broke from the line, charging as if they thought they faced a real enemy in the shape of Cherry, his camera and the little group of men around him. "Although I was in time to get a few feet of really excellent film, I felt quite glad when they were seized and disarmed."

Meanwhile, he secured some interesting pictures of Roosevelt as he watched the dance. The expression on his face made Cherry wonder if he was comparing it with scenes he must often have witnessed at American presidential elections. Roosevelt and Cherry trekked and camped together for several days.

Cherry's unique movie that including a lion hunt by Masai warriors was a sensation when screened in New York, raising enough money for him to be able to return to Africa in 1910. He was keen to photograph a lion hunt by the Masai, using spears, and he hired fifteen of the warriors for the purpose. Cherry's camera-bearer was put in charge of Cherry's fox terrier. One of the lions, driven by the warriors, took a course that would bring it near them. "The little terrier went mad with excitement. For some minutes she had been occupying all the boy's attention, straining at the leash, yapping and trying to break away and join in the fight against these great animals whose coughing growls and snarls must have stirred all her fighting and hunting instincts." As the breakaway lion passed at close quarters, the terrier snapped, not at the lion, which was out of her reach, but at the unfortunate camera-boy, who was trying to restrain her – and bit him in the leg!"

The lion took cover in bushes. Now the hunt had farcical aspects. Cherry proposed that he loosed his terrier, who would stand at the edge of the bushes and bark to flush the lion, which would then be dealt with by Masai spears. Instead, Pip dashed into the bushes, and straight at the lion, fixing sharp teeth in the lion's tail, hanging on to it. A spear put the pain-wracked lion out of its misery. So far, a photographic record of a lion hunt had not been made. Cherry tried again, with excellent results, the luckless lion dying at spear-point not far from the camera. Prepared for the screen, the film of the lion hunt had over the next few years an audience running into millions.

The most interesting of all the animals he saw during his African journeys was a chimpanzee which he filmed and projected to the world as "Toto". The chimp came from the Congo and his personality captured the hearts of thousands of natives who had never seen one of his kind.

# Jungle Days

IN 1911, Cherry was in Borneo and India. He was to recall Borneo for its dense jungle in which photography was virtually impossible, for the noisy profusion of life in the high tree-tops and for the "abominable canoes", consisting of trees hollowed out "at the cost of infinite labour and patience". Tropical thunderstorms were frightening. One night "all around us we could hear tree after tree crashing down; when there was a momentary lull every animal in the jungle seemed to be screaming with terror." He did manage to obtain the first movie shots of an orang utan in its native habitat.

He visited the Gormanton caves in which swifts nested in edible nests, "tens of thousands of which are collected every year and shipped to China... What child was ever taught that the Chinese ate birds'-nest soup and forgot the fact?" It was almost sundown when, wet through but with the cameras and films dry, they reached a small hut belonging to the firm that leased the caves from the government. "You can hang clothes out in the sun and put them to rights but it is not much use trying the same process with a wet film. Moreover, you can replace your stock of clothes or even, in an emergency, dispense with some of them; but in British North Borneo no new photographic apparatus was obtainable."

The first entrance was about four times the size of a railway tunnel. When Cherry and his companions reached it, swiftlets were flying in and out in swarms. The void was too large to permit for good photography, so Cherry lugged his camera and tripod up some hundred and fifty feet to the next entrance, which was but twice the size of a railway tunnel. Advised, before entering, to doff his boots to avoid slipping on the slope, Cherry did so. With a thunderstorm raging, the light was too bad to permit him to get good pictures of birds in massed flight. Flashlight photography of the interior was adopted. Shining his electric torch at the "carpet" of excreta, he saw "numbers of weird-looking grasshoppers" and, on a solitary rock, about a score of centipedes.

"At first the height of the caves seemed to be about sixty feet. Thousands upon thousands of nests were plastered over the roof. I tried to get a flash-light picture of these, after which we groped our way on for about another four hundred yards, the cave getting bigger all the time. Then, to my amazement, I saw what seemed to be little specks of light at least a hundred feet above the floor. Each of these lights, I found, represented a native collecting nests."

The nest-gatherers worked from ladders made of *rotan*, the jungle rope, suspended from the roof. It was dangerous work. "Many a native has been carried out of those caves limp and horrible, with every bone broken." The collectors operated at night so they would not be aware of the height. Cherry emerged from the underworld having taken some flashlight pictures.

He was determined to picture the birds flying in and about. He arranged for some food and blankets to be brought up. While he was waiting, he entered a hole which led to the great cave below. "More or less idly, I picked up a large stone and dropped it down the hole.

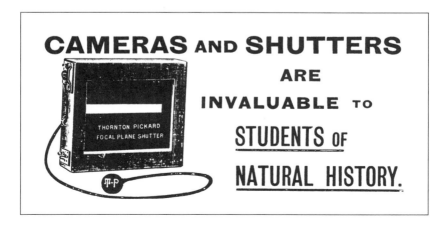

The effect was amazing. There was a rumble like thunder from the cavern and a moment later the birds and bats came out literally in thousands." At daybreak, as the swifts flew out, the hawks moved in and carried off many of the birds.

On his visit to India, he travelled through the forests on the back of an domesticated elephant. He also saw and was nearly over-whelmed by a charging herd of wild elephants. He went in search of the tiger, came across fresh pug-marks and evidence that a bullock had been taken and dragged by the tiger into densely-matted jungle. Foolishly, Cherry crawled through a tunnel in vegetation – "the tiger's private pathway" – and followed it until he came across some-thing dark crouching on the ground in front of him. It was the body of the bullock.

He returned to the area with the game warden and party of villagers. The warden stationed his men at intervals in a big circle. The men erected fencing by fixing poles upright in the ground and securing some heavy netting between them. Fires were lit so that the enclosed tiger was deterred from trying to force his way out. Cherry was invited to go into the cage, where he built a screen to provide cover for himself and his camera.

In due course, he came face to face with an animal he estimated to be fully eleven feet long and far bigger than any lion he had seen. The tiger, growling and snarling with anger at being disturbed, was "beautifully posed before me, giving its exhibition of ferocity at the beating of cans and the shouting behind it, and gazing straight into the lens – though fortunately without seeing either it or me. I have never in my whole life had a finer opportunity for a picture. The tiger stopped for a second, then it turned and disappeared. I was not alto-gether sorry to see it go."

# Pictures from Nature

A portfolio of photogravures by Richard and Cherry Kearton was published by Cassell in 1906. The pictures were chosen from over 10,000 negatives. "Our photographs have been secured from the interiors of stuffed oxen and sheep... and other re-assuring contrivances." The black-throated diver was photographed "on one of three hundred and sixty-five islands in a Hebridean loch."

**Leverets in their Form.** Gamekeepers were asked to report the finding of "leverets in their 'form' exactly where their mother had left them." It was arranged that if such was found, they were to "wire" the single word "Leverets" to Richard's office in Fleet Street. To obtain this photograph, he "rushed down to Ludgate Circus, caught a bus to St Pancras, and from there a train to Elstree, twelve miles away."

**Hedgehog.** To secure this photograph, Cherry focussed his camera on the animal, put a plate into position, fixed the longest piece of pneumatic tubing he owned to his focal plane shutter – and waited for the hedgehog to "unfurl and reveal his grizzly face." Nineteen times out of twenty, the animal did so while facing away from the camera.

**Sparrow Hawk at her Nest.** She was photographed while adding sticks to the structure, which was on the lower branches of a rowan tree growing on a steep hillside in the north-country. The hiding-tent from which the photograph was taken was covered with twigs and leaves. Patience was needed by the photographer, the weather being generally dull and wet.

**Ring Dove or Wood Pigeon.** This photograph was taken by Cherry one hot July day as he crouched in the "internal regions" of a "stuffed ox" with the lens of his camera peeping through a round hole in the hide, focused on bird visitors to a secluded pond. Instead of sipping, raising its head and allowing the water to trickle down its throat, the pigeon "thrust its bill deep into the pool and commenced to suck the water up like a horse."

**Peewit or Lapwing.** To obtain this superb study of a timid bird, Richard covered his hiding tent with rushes but made the mistake of entering the hide under the eyes of the birds. Next day, he went to the spot with a shepherd who, when he had seen Richard under cover, walked away. The deception was complete. He photographed her as she walked towards the nest.

*Right:* **Gannet or Solan Goose.**

# The New World

CHERRY visited Canada in 1912 as the guest of George Pratt, a member of the Camp Fire Club who had property in moose-country. Cherry saw few moose but "many, many dams where in former days the poor little beaver had worked so hard and so patiently to build his home and had been rewarded by having the poacher mark him down…"

In order to photograph a moose that was feeding in a lake, the two men, using a light canoe, attempted to get within photographic range. "The proper method is to work down with the sun behind you and paddle rapidly whilst the animal is under water; he, of course, being web-footed, can stand on the mud and actually walk on the bottom of the lake. He will remain down for something like half a minute, then come to the surface with the water streaming off his great head. Whilst he chews the food he has gathered in his mouth, he will gaze at you steadily; then, as though having decided that you are of no interest, he will sink out of sight again."

Several photographs were obtained of moose feeding – and moose dashing away when they discovered that the canoe contained a possible enemy. He obtained good pictures when, unaccountably, the great animal swam towards him. Cherry carried the canoe on his back from lake to lake. Mr Pratt took the food. He ate his dinner in the camp-fire smoke to be rid of mosquitoes.

Back in the United States, another North American friend, Dr Overton, took him to see the ospreys on Gardeners' Island, which was just off Long Island, having local fame as the spot where the first settlers landed. The osprey nests were dotted along the shore for about a mile and a half, usually with a hundred yards or so of space between them. The birds had young. Dr Overton had had an umbrella-shaped hiding-place constructed for his use, and Cherry spent half a day in it, his camera at the ready. He had no success. At another nest, he had "a kind of Red Indian wigwam constructed of some planks that had been washed up on the beach... The parent birds took no notice of the hiding-place and kept on visiting their offspring."

Cherry had close encounters with the brown bears of Yellowstone Park, some of which were looking for tourist refuse. He secured three hundred feet of film featuring a bear and her cub. "We passed numerous geysers and other fearsome holes full of boiling mud; in fact, the whole place was rumbling, spluttering and spouting." By the side of a place where his tent was pitched lay a small hot-water hole. "A kettle and a fire, the first necessities of an ordinary camp, seemed to be superfluous here. I soon discovered, however, that the chemicals in Yellowstone Park water turn everything red. When I attempted the development of some negatives, I discovered that even the emulsion went red and I had to cease my activities."

In 1913, Cherry was back in Africa, this time in the company of James Barnes. A full year was devoted to an expedition that ranged from coast to coast. They went to northern Kenya and set up their base camp some four miles from well-used waterholes where they recorded visits by reticulated giraffes, zebra, impala and other animals. They traversed Uganda and crossed the Congo border to take film of crocodiles on the Semliki River. Soon they were on the route, but moving in the opposite direction, that had been followed by the American explorer H M Stanley.

An account of an expedition to Central Africa, under the title *In the Land of the Lion*, published in 1929, was illustrated using 88 photographs, mostly taken from a cinematograph film produced by him for Cherry Kearton Films Ltd. The book was dedicated to Ada Kearton. Cherry dealt with the wildlife of an area of more than two hundred thousand square miles.

# Five Million Penguins

CHERRY'S BOOK, *The Island of Penguins*, published in 1930, told of his experiences while camping with Ada, and an attendant, in a vast nesting colony of Blackfooted or Jackass Penguins. Dassen Island, the temporary quarters for an estimated five million penguins, lay some thirty-five miles south of Cape Town, South Africa. In *Wild Life Across the World*, Cherry noted that when they arrived at Cape Town in the South African winter of 1921, the waiter at their hotel had presented them with penguin eggs for breakfast. The government authorities directed Cherry to the *Barracuta*, a "tub of a fishing boat", crewed by three, that would be sailing to the island in a few days for a cargo of penguin eggs.

The *Barracuta*, "all deck and hold", set sail at midnight. The quarters were constricted and smelly from an old paraffin engine. A storm swept the area and the skipper turned back, to attempt a crossing on the following night in something of the same conditions. This time they got as far as Robin Island, a leper colony. Once again, the skipper turned back. He was not going to be beaten and sailed again, at one-thirty in the morning, on a night even worse than the other two. "Our little boat was turned, twisted and tossed about like a cork."

For a third time, they returned to harbour. The skipper decided to make another attempt in daylight. When the boat was a few miles out, the sail was raised to steady the boat. The boat narrowly missed the reefs at Penguin Island. They sailed through a wall of spray and, finding a passage way, entered smoother water.

In *The Island of Penguins*, Cherry tells how the visitors were rowed in a small boat to the beach in a sheltered bay, where the reception committee consisted of about a thousand of the birds. The Keartons occupied a tent pitched on a tract of vacant earth with nesting burrows on every side of it. The penguins were to disturb their sleep.

"Imagine yourself in the centre of a field in which are tethered a hundred donkeys. And then imagine those donkeys all braying at the same moment."

Penguins constantly wandered into the tent out of curiosity or to steal. "They reared their families practically on our doorstep; they quarrelled, fought, moulted and made love on every side of us… I met the proud and the meek, the bully, the mischief-maker, the comfortable old gentleman, the despised weakling and the social outcast. I saw weddings, fights, the tragic collapse of a house, fun at the seaside – every happening almost that would provide a headline in our newspapers if it occurred in London or New York…"

Cherry had the ability to impart information about wildlife in an entertaining way. As, for example, in his chapter headed "Sharks". Every evening shoals of large fish came into the bay at the Island of Penguins. For an hour or more there would be a great deal of swimming and plunging, with a noise that could be heard a hundred yards away. He was puzzled by the excitement until he was aware that sharks were using the bay as a trap in which to catch fish. A shoal of fish driven into the bay was at their mercy.

Late one night, after the noise had abated, he filled a bucket with dead fish and went far out along the shelving rocks, then threw the dead fish into the sea. As the fish sank, the water flurried and an ugly black head rose in the darkness. Cherry instantly knew what might have happened if he, and not a bucket full of dead fish, had fallen in the sea.

Reviewers of *The Island of Penguins* were entranced. S P B Mais, writing in *The Daily Telegraph*, commented: "Like all Mr Kearton's work, it is quite wonderfully illustrated with close-up photographs and written with a verve and humour that are quite inimitable. These photographs keep one in a state of continuous hilarity."

# Continental Interludes

IN JUNE, 1911, Richard and his friend Howard Bentham – who was to become his son-in-law – visited the Dovre Feld in Norway. They recruited Norwegian helpers with inevitable difficulties over language, though Richard undoubtedly recognised some of the words. He had been born and reared in an area of the Yorkshire Dales that was colonised by Norse folk and some of their expressions lingered in the dialect.

Nesting in firs not far from their hotel were fieldfares, the frosty-voiced, grey-patched thrushes of the northern forests. Their *chack chacking* notes of protest were to be heard whenever anyone came near their nests and, as Richard observed, "it was immaterial whether the intruder was a peaceful peasant woman who passed every morning enticing her cows into the forest to graze or a troublesome photographer who climbed every tree containing a nest."

The redwing, cousin of the fieldfare, nested in isolated pairs "like its relative, the song thrush." Individual birds were heard calling in haunts at an elevation of over 4,000 ft, "where the birch trees appeared to be giving up the struggle for existence and old snowdrifts were plentiful." First attempts to find a nest were unsuccessful. Then a nest was located in a depression on the ground after the visitors had hidden themselves and kept watch on a demonstrative female. The nest, which contained five eggs, consisted of dead grass stems, lined with finer dead grass. "In the absence of the eggs it could not have been distinguished from a ring-ouzel's nest."

Anxious not to reveal the nest to the local hooded crows, Richard took several pictures of it and then draped it with pieces of juniper. The bird returned to brood. A hide was erected and Richard used its cover and waited for the return of the redwing, but the bird appeared to be upset by a glint of light from the camera lens and flew off, uttering her "somewhat thrush-like alarm notes". In contrast, the male bird "charged the lens in angry rushes but upon arriving within a foot or two of it rose into the air, passed over the hide and alighted on a tree behind."

Eventually, the female was back on the nest and Richard's camera was set to work. He exposed two or three plates in quick succession but later discovered the plates were over-exposed. His dreams were tormented by images of the hooded crows robbing the nest so, between five and six o' clock next morning, he left the hotel with his camera, heading for the redwing nest. His plans were thwarted by a wandering bull, which approached, snorting, causing him to take refuge behind a decrepit fence.

When the bull thrust his head through a hole in the fence, Richard picked up a fencing stake, whirled it in a circle, and brought it down with a crash on the bull's nose. The dazed bull took some time to recover, then spent some of its fury on a peat-bank before departing, "slowly it is true, and stopping ever and anon to look back and bawl an angry challenge." When, after breakfast, he entered the hide, the redwings behaved splendidly. The bull was not seen again. Ten days later, Richard re-located the nest, which now held young birds. Hastily he re-erected his hide and next day obtained "two hundred feet of beautiful film."

A willow grouse was brooding a family of down-clad young. "The old bird sprang from the short heather at my feet… mounted the air for a yard or so, then came down as if she had been shot and began to scuffle round me in ever-widening circles, feigning an inability to fly, whilst her chicks scattered… After some little trouble, I managed to catch a couple, and although they made anything but tractable sitters I exposed two or three plates upon them before they finally escaped…" Richard reflected that if the willow grouse lived on the heather-clad hills of Scotland, it would be difficult to distinguish its eggs or young ones from those of the red grouse. "The crowing notes of the adult males of the two species are, to my ears, identical in every respect." (The red grouse is now regarded as an island form of the widely-distributed willow grouse).

Richard was keen to photograph a snow bunting "and arriving at a place called Kongsvold, situated at the foot of a mountain, rising by a gentle slope to an elevation of some six thousand feet above sea level, judged it a likely spot to find what I required." His companion, to whom he was introduced by his landlady, was "a benevolent-looking old gentleman" and their conversation was limited to "vell" and "ja" or "na". After much trudging, they sat down in a wilderness of grey weatherworn crags, on the summit of the mountain, to eat their lunch.

The old man sang for a while then lit his pipe. Richard was too uncomfortable even to whistle for though it was July, a chilling wind seemed to go through him like a knife. He found the silence oppressive. "Presently, a low, sweet bird note caught my ear." It was a snow bunting. A cock bird was sitting on a boulder on the far side of a deep rock-strewn ravine. When the song ended, the bird flew towards the visitors and alighted on a patch of grass a few yards away, picking up tit bits of food before approaching a hole about a hundred yards from where Richard was sitting and from which the female bird left.

Richard thrust his hand into the hole and, contrary to expectation, found that the nest contained eggs. The male had been feeding the brooding female. Richard built a stone wall for concealment and signalled to the old man to move out of sight. He then rolled himself in his tent cloth and awaited the return of the bunting. When this did not happen, he turned to find the old man sitting on a knoll a few paces away. When the old chap was persuaded to depart, Richard exposed two or three plates as the hen bird rushed into her nesting hole.

From the high mountains to the low shoreline of Holland was a transition that Richard accomplished towards the end of May, 1914. He and daughter Grace visited Holland to study the breeding birds of the *polders* and *meers*. Their Dutch friends, Monsieur and Madame Burdet, took them to the island of Texel which had become a popular haunt for English bird-photographers. For example, Jasper Atkinson, of Leeds, was there to show them a redshank nest with scanty cover. Richard contrasted this with the well-concealed nest of the redshank on the Pennines.

Richard and Grace put up a hide on an avocet nest and were dismayed when one egg was devoured by a scholekster [oystercatcher]. The camera was subsequently focussed on an oystercatcher scrape containing eggs, the brooding bird being "so courageous we could hardly drive her away…" Grace took some still photographs, then Richard moved in with his cinematograph to record the female flying off with a fragment of egg-shell in its bill shortly after one of her chicks had hatched.

The so-called Kentish plover was numerous. Ruffs displayed on "hills" that had been used from time immemorial and were now being driven from one roadside site by passing walkers or vehicles. At rare intervals a reeve, the female of the species, would alight upon the scene and remain for a few moments an almost indifferent spectator leading to speculation that, this being late in the season, she had left her nest to feed and look around.

A small green hiding tent was set up near the tuft of grass containing the nest of a pair of black-tailed godwits. The duty bird refused to accept the tent, so it was covered with reeds. The bird promptly returned to brood. "Curiously, out of a whole series of photographs taken of this bird standing near her nest or in the act of sitting on her eggs, there is hardly one that does not carry the suggestion of a stuffed specimen. Her awkwardness and stiffness whilst watching the lens was no doubt due, to some extent, to nervousness." Black terns nested in the grass, alongside common terns and black-headed gulls. Grace and another English friend, G Booth, set up their "little photographic tents" near a colony of black terns, one of the pair being acutely shy and the other attacking the hide whenever the photographer stirred inside it.

Richard's son John, who was born in 1900, often assisted his father with photographic work and eventually became a bird photographer, writing and illustrating two natural history books.

# The Great War

IN THE spring of 1914, when the proverbial war clouds were gathering, Richard Kearton and his friend Howard Bentham, a great authority on the Dartford warbler, found a nest containing well grown young in deep heather far away from any furze bushes, in which this rare species was normally found. Patiently, Richard tamed the adult female until it would light on his hand to feed a fledgling. The bird had three young. During two days of observation the cock bird was not seen near the nest.

Richard and all the family, staying at Nateby, travelled over to Swaledale by horse-drawn coach, though father and sons walked up the steep road to Tailbrigg to ease the work of the horses. They stayed at Muker with John R Fawcett and his mother. Visiting Neddy Dick at Keld, they heard him play a "stone instrument " formed using beck-bottom stones of various sizes, Neddy tapped them like a xylophone. Neddy's eccentricity was evident when, inheriting some silver plate from a relative he did not like, he tossed it into the river. On that pre-war jaunt, the Keartons joined in singing *John Peel* before walking up Iveletside to look at the lead mines in Swinnergill. Richard found a piece of rock on which was imprinted the outline of a fern.

War brought with it the threat of air attacks. Richard had grown up as the once-great Pennine lead-mining industry came to an end. He had used his knowledge of mining to dig a tunnel under the chalk lawn at the family home, Ashdene, in the Caterham Valley of Surrey. The tunnel was a useful shelter when zeppelins were overhead.

The garden was turned to vegetable production and in one year two tons of potatoes were harvested. Richard, keeping two pigs and some poultry, remarked: "I fed my intelligent and affectionate animals, washed out their abode every day and welcomed... two small pensioners – a robin and a mouse – that lived mainly on the unconsidered trifles to be picked up in and around my sty."

Richard was asked by the Navy if he could train seabirds to help spot submarines. This was not possible. Years later, someone else was to try with no better luck.

He was ever-aware of the natural world. While waiting in the open air for an expected zeppelin raid, he noted that farmyard roosters, pheasants, partridges, peewits and other birds began to call "long before the ominous whir of the invaders' propellers became audible to the most sensitive human ears."

Cherry Kearton, having journeyed across Africa, returned to England in June 1914. He was a director and the largest shareholder in a small company called The Warwick Trading Co., which produced Britain's first film gazette. Topical events were filmed and put on public display. Cherry was bubbling over with unusual ideas. When the King and Queen visited France, film was "shot" of the King inspecting a guard of honour in Dover at noon and then Cherry arranged for Huck, a famous airman, to carry one of the company's operators to obtain aerial pictures of the royal ship as it crossed the Channel. Film was then obtained of the royal couple landing in Calais. The hired aircraft flew the film back to Hendon – and it was screened at the *Coliseum* at 4-30 that same afternoon.

With the outbreak of war, the filmsters leapt at the chance of making a supplement to their gazette entitled *The Whirlpool of War*, being first screened at the *Palace Theatre*. Cherry offered his services to the Flying Corps but the ranks had already been filled. He applied to the War Office for a job. They had no vacancies. The upshot was that he took an active part in filming for *The Whirlpool of War*, visiting Belgium weekly, and making his way by car to various parts of the Line. He was sometimes so close to the action, he risked being captured by the enemy.

Cherry observed heart-rending sights in Belgium. Here were long streams of refugees, with young wives pushing barrows on which were piled up the least bulky objects they had managed to salvage from their homes and with one or two small children perched on top, while older children ran along clinging to their mother's skirts, the old grandparents trudging behind. He met an old man, alone, "who came uncertainly down the road, stopping twice to look behind him as if he doubted there was any point in trying to live."

As Cherry filmed shells bursting against a church tower in a deserted Belgium town, he felt more lonely than he had been in Africa or on the moors of his native Yorkshire. Coming across the body of a man lying across a pavement, he took a closer look and started in amazement. "This unknown Belgium was the exact double of myself – height, build, features and even clothes were exactly the same!" An English girl, serving as a nurse with an ambulance, asked Cherry if he had a piece of string. She wanted to hang a still-warm piece of shell from her neck "for luck". When Antwerp came under the pressure of the German advance, and shells rained on the city, Cherry exposed a thousand feet of film in twenty-four hours.

Cherry then returned to East Africa and to service with the Legion of Frontiersmen – the 25th Royal Fusiliers. He served with several former big-game hunters, led by Colonel Driscoll, "a born soldier and leader of men." Cherry and F C Selous (then sixty-four years of age) became Driscoll's intelligence officers in a unit that was concentrated at Kajaido, half-way between the Uganda Railway and the Magadi Soda Lake in the game reserve. An intimate connection with natural history began when someone stole Cherry's bed, forcing him to sleep on the ground. When he awoke and shook his sleeping-bag, from it fell a scorpion, a centipede and a hairy caterpillar, "none of them of the type a wise man chooses for bedfellows."

On a fourteen day patrol to discover where the Germans obtained water when trekking to blow up the Uganda Railway, the party of which Cherry was a member found the stream and traced it to where it sank in the sandy bottom of a small donga. "I photographed it with a small stereo-camera – and then we went on." A man who went scouting on his hands and knees came face to face with a cobra, which after a short while – during which the two stared unblinkingly at one another – crawled away. At an outpost, a company of soldiers was alerted by a cry "Look out, they're rushing us!" They opened fire on what turned out to be a troop of baboons. Cherry began a collection of beetles, his friend Selous taking an interest in butterflies.

Cherry took charge of an aerodrome in enemy territory. Under his care were five mechanics and some thirty native porters whose work consisted in looking after the petrol stores and effecting repairs to visiting aircraft. Lions visited a nearby mud-hole to drink. Of the campaign, Cherry wrote: "We were fighting 'open warfare' with a far-flung battle line… We frequently marched without water and were often short also of rations. There was a lack of proper and adequate medical supplies and the danger of sudden and devastating outbreaks of fever and dysentry was always with us." After several years, he was sent home to recuperate.

Richard observed to his family when the Great War was over: "We will be paying for it for the rest of our lives." In the spring of 1919, he listened to a blackbird that had incorporated in its song three notes from a tune popular with Canadian soldiers who whistled it in and around a nearby training camp. The songs of some birds might be translated into human phrases. "To me that of the chaffinch always sounds exactly like the words *see, see, see, Joe Dobson's very near.*"

Soon after the Armistice, Cherry was invited by the War Office to lecture among the British troops in Belgium and Germany. He recounted his experiences before the King and Queen at Windsor

Castle. He went diamond-hunting in South Africa without success, renewed his acquaintance with the Sahara and explored Algeria.

In *The Shifting Sands of Algeria*, published in 1924, Cherry wrote of a land he had first visited early in the century. He mentioned its "smooth and excellent governing by the French" and some of the lesser-known creatures, such as processional caterpillars and trap-door spiders. When he visited the "mountain men", he heard of a snake with hair or mane along its back, which never ran away but gave chase at great speed. It was the third time in his life he had missed seeing such a snake about which various informants had confidently told him in Borneo and in North and Central Africa. "Of course, there may be something in what these Arabs told me. They, at any rate, do not see snakes through the neck of a whisky bottle."

Of course, he met the Arabian camel, "a very stout-built fellow, splendidly constructed for carrying loads." His hump was supposed to be used for storing water, which was not correct. None the less, the hump had its uses. "It stores fat." Cherry asked the guide why his camel looked so supercilious. "His answer was because he can see the other camel's hump but cannot see his own." A camel could digest almost anything. A favourite food in Algeria was halfa-grass, but "he can eat thorn branches, date palm leaves and the coarsest of grasses and thistles and, most wonderful of all, he seems to like the foliage of the prickly pear, a plant introduced from America into Algeria and now much used there for making hedges."

# Magic Lantern and Cinematograph

NO MAN has been more successful in bringing fresh air onto a lecture platform than Richard Kearton. Adventures he had shared with Cherry, and which had led to the publication of the trail-blazing *With Nature and a Camera*, had an echo in winter when he gave illustrated lectures. His lectures stressed the pleasures to be found in bird-watching – pleasures that might be enjoyed by all. When he was invited to broadcast by the BBC he declined. He liked to work a lecture to a climax point and felt he could not put it over in the same way on radio. The projector, still invariably known as a "magic lantern", was eventually superseded by the cinematograph. Richard kept his faith in lantern slides to the end and considered there was no real future for "movies".

It was his forceful personality that people were to remember. He loved a live audience and spoke from experience. He was no academic. Many of the slides had been hand-tinted by his wife or by daughter Grace and drew applause from large audiences who had seen him limp on to a platform and, within minutes, were responding warmly to his stories of his experiences of Nature, some happy, some grave, spiced with laconic north-country wit and humour.

On the more splendid occasions, Richard was expected to lecture in full evening dress. His adaptation of this was somewhat strange, consisting only of a black coat which he wore with the garments in which he had travelled. It was his boast that he never wore a suit that would prevent his climbing to investigate a bird's nest. In all the years he was lecturing – and that career began in 1897, during the golden age of the magic lantern – his garb never changed. Nor did the freshness of his presentation.

He was fond of recalling a visit to the Outer Hebrides, when he stayed with a doctor friend. He mentioned to the doctor that when he was young, enjoying a fishing trip to Armathwaite, on the River Eden, he sallied forth to dig worms for bait. An old keeper demonstrated how to do it with little effort. He drove the prongs of the fork into the ground at an angle of about 75 degrees, then tapped gently on the handle with the palm of his hand. The ground vibrated. A number of worms appeared on the surface and glided away in different directions, as though escaping from a mole.

Richard tried the experiment in various parts of Britain, nearly always successfully. On that trip to the Outer Hebrides he arranged a demonstration to support the old notion. It worked. Said the doctor: "Unfortunately for your theory, there has never been a mole on this island, so far as anyone knows, since the world began."

Richard told Frank Lowe: "When I was young I carried my bag. Now I am old, I can ride." The man who had become the most sought-after lecturer in the land showed his nature slides to the royal children at Sandringham, and took slides into prisons and asylums. He lectured in every town and village of any size in England, also in Paris and Berlin. Returning from Berlin in 1912, he told the family that the Germans were talking of nothing else but "the mailed fist and shining armour". He was certain they were intent on war. He was invited to lecture in America, as the guest of "Teddy" Roosevelt. Grace treasured an autographed photograph that this vigorous and genial president sent to her father.

After several weeks of touring, his slides and films became somewhat careworn. Grace patiently repaired and cleaned hundreds of slides and rejoined the films broken by heat or careless lanternists. He was meticulous in his preparation and insisted that if a moving picture lecture was chosen, a fireproof iron chamber must be provided.

A presentation called *The Fairyland of Nature*, available as a slide talk or as "moving pictures", showed rooks fighting over food, titmice going through their gymnastic displays, a green woodpecker taking a bath, tail first, in a cattle pond and a hedgehog and her young. Also on view was the caterpillar of a swallow-tailed butterfly changing into a chrysalis. Slides only, or slides and films, were available in the show entitled *Joy of the Open Air*. In this, the audience saw the flowers of spring and were introduced to "the mysterious habits of the cuckoo" and "why foxes fail to find sitting partridges and pheasants until the young ones are hatched", this being an introduction to cryptic colouration.

In *Nature at Work and Play* (slides only), Richard posed a good number of questions, asking if a sparrow hawk builds its own nest, if frogs cry out when scared and "do young birds go to school"? He showed sexton beetles at work burying a dead rat and dealt with "a bird that puzzled Gilbert White [a pioneer field observer] and how the lecturer photographed a member of the species in a field tenanted by a mad bull."

Meanwhile, Cherry enthralled large crowds with his wildlife films. They included *My Dog Simba, Wild Life Across the World, In the Land of the Lion* and his autobiographical film, *The Big Game of Life*. His film *Dassen* was "shot" during three months spent on an island off Cape Town that bore the name and was the home of the penguin colony.

His movie film *With Cherry Kearton in the Jungle* received the honour of a Royal command. *Tembi* featured, among other African creatures, Lutembe, the sacred crocodile of Lake Victoria. In producing *Tembi* he had travelled twelve thousand miles through Central Africa, his wife Ada – who had a slight knowledge of local dialects – acting as "stage manager" to the native actors.

A programme that accompanied the film gave a potted biography of "the man behind the camera". The lion dominating the screen towards the end of the story was filmed at a range of twenty feet!

Nateby

Kirkby Stephen

Westmorland

16/6/26

My Dear Frank

Many thanks for your nice long letter of the 9th inst sent on to me here. I am glad to hear of all your doings but could wish your luck had been greater.

I came North with Jack thinking it would benefit my health and that I could be of some assistance but fear that neither hope has been justified. My enlarged heart kicks against

A letter to Frank Lowe, of Bolton, by Richard Kearton.

the climbing of these forbidding hills and our luck from an ornithological point of view has been of the poorest.

I have known this neighbourhood (my mother's country) all my life but never remember it in such a poverty stricken condition from a bird point of view. I have not seen a single Redstart or heard a single Corncrake and nearly everything we have found has been robbed by I strongly suspect Rooks or Jackdaws. Jack has only been able to make a series of a Golden Plover & Sandpiper at the nest in a fortnight! What do you think of that for poor going? We are now waiting for the weather

to clear up a bit before we tackle a
Grey Wagtail in a rather poor place;
then if I'm fit enough we shall
go over the hills into Yorkshire
and have a peep at my old home.
  The strike has played the very
deuce with everything. My Autobiography
was doing well up to the stoppage
but was then of course brought to
an absolute standstill. It is going
again now and my youngest boy
who is in a Literary Agency in
London has sold a small Edn
to an American Publisher. The
reviews have been excellent & I
have had scores and scores of
congratulatory letters from known
and unknown friends upon the book.
Yes indeed as you say in your P.P.S
it is nice to hear of people
who remember one's long past

dealings with them as a pleasure.
I reckon its the right way to live
life.

A cousin of mine living near
Burnley is very anxious that I
should spend a day or two in
that neighbourhood on my way back
from Yorks and if the state
of my health permits I shall
do so and endeavour to call on
you during my journey South.

I brought my trout rod North
with me intending to do a bit of fishing
but have not been able to try my
hand yet.

Pray excuse the disjointed
brevity of this note and Believe
me Dear Frank with all good
wishes for your continued Success
Your Very Faithfully
R. Kearton

# Richard's Story

RICHARD had a hand in over 20 books. His autobiography, published in 1926, was described by the *Morning Post* as "the revelation of a delightful personality". Punch gave its review in verse:

> *Here a real romance is told*
> *(Fact in this form fiction betters)*
> *How a herd-boy left the fold,*
> *How he won a place in letters;*
> *Loving much, beloved of Pan –*
> *Bird and beast and fellow man.*

Richard wrote: "My object in writing the story of my life was to encourage the young and amuse the old. It is gratifying to know that success has crowned my humble efforts in both directions. Hundreds of warm-hearted letters and press reviews supply undeniable proof of the fact. Some readers tell me they have been inspired and others that they have been amused. One gentleman flatters me and at the same time strains my credulity by boldly asserting that he has read the volume through three times."

But life did not end with an autobiography. He was absorbed by bird and animal life around his Surrey home, where he had first heard the nightingale singing and, enchanted, stayed up all night to listen. "The bird sings as blithely by day as by night, but his notes are, in the ears of the inexperienced, mixed up and obscured by those of such accomplished performers as the blackcap warbler, the garden warbler, song thrush and the flute-like utterances of the blackbird."

Frank Lowe, visiting Richard Kearton at his Surrey home, mentioned that he had never heard a nightingale. At once, Richard pulled on his boots and together they walked up Godstone Hill, where a cock bird was singing. Frank recalled that Richard's delight in introducing him to this south-country bird was as great as his joy in hearing it for the first time. Another day, Richard showed Frank a colony of pipistrelle bats that had taken up residence at the corner of a lintel above a doorway that led into the garden. Richard drew his guest's attention to the peculiar odour exuded by the bats – and to the small heaps of bat-dung on the ground below the hole.

Richard's son John was absent from home on many occasions as he followed his natural history interests. In the early 1920s, he was in West Africa. At home, Richard's daughter Grace took over most of the "still" photography while her father concentrated on making cine films. Richard's lame foot was supported by a large cork boot and he found scrambling somewhat arduous. It was his son Cherry's task to see that the cork boot was efficiently polished before his father set out on his innumerable lecture tours. Grace was to recall: "Few people ever knew he was so lame. From a swinging walk he used I could tell his step on the path as he returned about 1 a.m. by the last train from an engagement near London."

Friends in the north mentioned a possible knighthood for Richard as an acknowledgement of his services to natural history. When he declined to think of such an honour, Grace wondered if he was troubled with the thought of having to kneel to accept the accolade. His bad knee could not be properly bent. (Grace, when she was over eighty years of age, could still "hear" in her mind her father's distinctive tread on those late returns to the house. The sound was to be inseparably linked in her thoughts with the hooting of owls in the distance).

Father and daughter took it in turns to tuck each other in the hides used for photography. They set up a hide near the nest of a pair of Dartford warblers. The birds were feeding young and the female was an unusually confiding bird. When the chicks were close to fledging,

Richard removed one from the nest, sat down with outstretched legs with the chick on one knee and was delighted when a parent bird flew down and fed it. The incident was photographed and appeared in a book.

Grace recalled: "He had a great love for the birds themselves. Modern naturalists tend to regard them without sentiment. I knew him to get up one night in the middle of a heavy rainstorm to walk down a long garden to a thrush nest. He took with him an old trilby hat and used it to cover the nest. Next morning he had the joy of finding mother bird and her young quite dry under the old hat. If he found young in a nest, under some circumstances he would tuck them inside his shirt to keep them warm until mother came back."

Richard's son, Cherry, helped to carry the heavy cameras to out-of-the-way places and to cover the tent used as a hide with fresh-cut saplings. "Father often had a long wait for a bird to return to the nest. I would fall asleep and awaken to hear his stentorian voice shouting: 'Where the devil is that boy'?"

Unknown to most of his fans, Richard was a keen shot. His sport was with rabbits and any game birds that showed their beaks in the neighbourhood. Richard and the local doctor, who were great friends, devoted Boxing Day to their sport. (Richard's shotgun was one of the old hammer type. It hung for years on a wall in the lounge at Cherry's home. In 1940, at the start of a second world war, he offered it to the Local Defence Volunteers. It was returned as being useless).

# Changing Times

LIVING IN Surrey, Richard missed "the clear cool springs and prattling becks" of his native area. He wrote in 1915: "In Caterham Valley we have no running streams except for the intermittent 'bourne' or 'woe-water'. The heaviest downpour of rainwater sinks deep down into the chalk beds and bubbles up again in clear springs on the southern side of the Downs."

He was well out of range of the crowing of red grouse and the "plain call note" of the golden plover. There were compensations. The ringing laugh of the yaffle, or green woodpecker, was heard in the not-far-distant timber belts and was, according to local weather lore, a sure indication that rain was on the way. Richard also felt that "the sweet cadences of the silver-tongued woodlark" was hard to beat.

On his Surrey moor, on still evenings, he heard the curious trilling song of the nightjar, also known as goatsucker or fern owl. While passing through a wood he knew well, he would see what appeared to be a piece of dead bark lying on the ground. A closer inspection revealed a nightjar, "covering her pair of pebble-like eggs." Richard was fond of "calling" the cuckoo. If he hid himself and produced "any kind of colourable imitation of his notes, during the month of May especially," the cuckoo might be lured to close quarters and return the calls.

During the early months of the year, Richard Kearton prepared for the nesting season by dispersing potential nesting places – items of junk such as old coffee-pots, jam-jars, kettles and biscuit-boxes, some of which would be used by robins. Two broods were reared in a coffee-pot and another brood hatched out in the lower half of a stone beer-bottle lying on its side. One pair of robins nested in a jam jar.

The main predator was the prowling cat. Richard's love for the wild mammalia of his garden did not extend to a neighbour's pet.

The Ashdene household always kept a well-supplied bird table and this cat threatened to use it as a baited trap for small birds. Richard shot at a stone a foot away from the cat; the rattle of the stone so startled it that it vanished from sight, never to return. At a farmstead in Greater London, where the housewife loved her cats, Richard countered by partly burying  small uncorked bottles of liquid ammonia near the nests of the remaining robins, plus those of hedge sparrow and blackbird. Here he photographed a robin's nest in a basket, a great tit returning to its nest inside the spout of a disused pump and a wren's nest in a coil of rope that hung, otherwise unwanted, in an outhouse.

He kept a diary, which was a useful source of material for books and articles and, when he was ill towards the end of his life, a consolation, enabling him to re-live many of his experiences. An example was when, studying birdlife in the Outer Hebrides, he had erected his "hide" on a dunlin and, leaving the hide to remove an offending blade of grass in the foreground, found to his delight that the disturbed bird ran no more than a few feet and had returned to the nest  before he settled behind the camera for another spell of photography.

When there was an overnight deluge, which flooded the nest and drowned a new-hatched chick, Richard re-arranged the nest so it was above water level and replaced three eggs that were chipping and thus on the point of hatching. A day or two afterwards, as he watched the dunlin chicks with their parents, a skylark picked up "some edible item of food" and tried to give it to one of the young dunlin, much to the annoyance of one of the parents.

In the summer of 1920, visiting the northern fell-country with an assistant, Richard spent several days exposing still and cine film at a ring ouzel nest in a north-country gill. (Other ouzel pairs nested down shakeholes, which are funnel-shaped, caused where the earth has been shaken or washed down into some cavity in the limestone rock). The hen bird was running a shuttle-service with food; the cock bird was conspicuous by its absence.

Several hundred yards away, a blackbird was incubating eggs in a nest which, surprisingly, had been built in rough grass, away from any bush or tree. Directly her chicks were hatched, she disappeared. Her mate fed and brooded the family. The answer to these unusual events came when he found that a tawny owl was nesting in a hollow tree. Beside the owlets was evidence of its predation on other birds.

At about the same time, Richard watched a carrion crow hunting a rough, bent-clad pasture on a Westmorland fellside. It flushed a grouse from her nest; then, catching sight of Richard, sheered off. "Although baulked for the moment, this sable marauder had evidently made careful mental notes of its find." The clutch of eggs diminished at the rate of one egg a day.

As a change from fell-country, Richard and his assistant travelled to Ravenglass, at the mouth of the River Esk in what is now Cumbria. They had a hurried evening meal, then made straight for the small whitewashed cottage of an old friend, Joe Farren, boatman. Joe's cottage was found to be empty and dissolute. Richard wrote in his diary that he had departed into the Silences (Joe was occupying his little cottage by the estuary when the author called in the early 1950s. Joe recalled when he rowed the Keartons across to Drigg Point, the nesting place of gulls and terns).

On Drigg, Richard and his assistant walked on a path through an area of teeming bird life to where there were Sandwich terns. "On the shore, some two hundred yards away, we found a huge conical hamper half-buried in the sand, so dug it up and utilised it as a hiding contrivance. When inverted there was plenty of room under-neath for photographer and apparatus. I cut a round hole through the wickerwork on one side for my lens to look through and another at the back for signalling purposes."

He was duly installed. The tern with the nearest nest returned without a trace of fear or suspicion. Richard obtained "a beautiful series of pictures of her on and near her handsome pair of eggs." He then signalled with his handkerchief to his assistant that the session was over. They returned next morning with a "moving-picture camera". The hamper was moved back so the tern would not be at the same large scale and would more readily accept the situation. Alas, the bird in question had a neighbour two or three feet away that had just hatched out two chicks. She took charge of one while the female cared for the other. Everyone was happy except the photographer.

During the last few years of his life, in the 1920s, he managed periodically to return to his natal area. While resting on a peat bank one hot day in the spring of 1922, he heard the low, sweet notes of the dunlin, a favourite bird, known to Pennine shepherds and gamekeepers as *judcock*. In less than half an hour, Richard saw the female return to a nest under a trailing bunch of dead bent grass. The nest held four eggs. Richard's ability to remain still and quiet for long periods meant that during the course of one morning the dunlin and he became well acquainted with each other. He took "a whole gallery of still and moving pictures."

Richard was unlucky with a pair of golden plover on a bare part of the fell, known locally as *smittle-grund*. The golden plover does not care for rank vegetation. "A friendly shepherd found a nest for me… far below what I would have called the breeding line of the species, but to my great regret another equally friendly keeper of sheep drove his flock right over it on the evening of the same day, broke two of the beautiful eggs and made the bird forsake."

That same year he located a brown owl in a limestone cave and a pair of ring-ouzels in a shakehole. It was a bad year for farming. He saw the "sickening sights" of sheep being eaten alive by maggots. Richard associated this with the decline in the number of lapwings, which had consumed vast quantites of insects pests. Lapwing eggs were being sold in London restaurants.

At home, he had a trickle of naturalist visitors. Norman Ellison, who became Nomad, the wildlife wanderer of BBC *Children's Hour*, wrote to Richard Kearton early in 1927 asking advice on publishing some nature notes. By return post came a reply from a man who had only a year to live. Richard wrote: "A thousand thanks for your kind and interesting letter. Pray do not talk about 'taking a liberty' in writing to me. When my heart has grown too cold to take an interest in the observations of any fellow student of nature, I shall not be Dicky Kearton and it will be high time it stopped beating."

He offered the desired advice and added: "You cannot tell what a joy letters like yours are to me now that I am a broken old man. My health gave way just over a year ago and I am now left with a 'groggy' heart and excessive blood pressure. You can imagine what a caterpillar diet and locomotion restricted to that of a sick snail mean to a man of buoyant spirits and untiring energy. Ah well, I've had an uncommonly good time and am not complaining. It's a great thing to be assured, by friends one has never met, of help and good healthy pleasures given."

In 1924, he was at a family wedding at Kirkby Stephen, chatting with his relatives, lapsing into the old Dales dialect. Writing to Frank Lowe from the old home at Nateby in the summer of 1926, he observed that he had travelled North with his son Jack, for health reasons and in the hope he might be of some assistance to his son in his bird photography but "neither hope has been justified. My enlarged heart kicks against the climbing of those forbidding hills and our luck from an ornithological point of view has been of the poorest."

He had known the Nateby area – "my mother's country" – all his life but "have not seen a single Redstart or heard a single Corncrake and nearly everything we have found has been robbed by, I strongly suspect, Rooks or Jackdaws."

*Muker School, where plaques to the memory of Richard and Cherry Kearton were unveiled.*

# Cherry Goes "Down Under"

CHERRY, his brother, continued to live a full and varied life. Quite tall, burly, flamboyant, he would occasionally return to Swaledale on the back seat of a chauffeur-driven car, with his wife Ada, and stay at the guest house in Muker own by David Harker, an old school friend, who called Cherry "a rum lad".

Cherry believed in "getting on" and was fond of saying "always look upwards". He was driven over Buttertubs Pass, intent in making a film about peat-digging. He was seen in the crowd at Muker Show. His account of the five months he spent on Penguin Island, off South Africa, published in 1930, was dedicated "to the memory of Dick, my dear brother and comrade over many rough roads."

There was time for a last big adventure – in Java, Australia and New Zealand – recorded in his book *I Visit the Antipodes*. The trip took place in 1937 and the book appeared a year later. He dedicated it to Captain Cook, knowing how the great Yorkshire circumnavigator must have felt "when, having faced almost uncharted seas on his way to unknown lands, he thought of the Yorkshire moorlands he had left behind."

Cherry and Ada sailed from England with photographic equipment that was considerably less bulky than his original camera and accessories. The Keartons were "in search of the sun and any adventure which might be lurking about". In Australia, they hoped during their travels to remain incognito but were recognised – and greeted effusively – by another celebrity, the writer, Zane Grey.

Visiting the zoo at Melbourne, Cherry picked up and nursed a young koala bear – "a winsome little Teddy". Ada, anxious to take a photograph, shouted his name to attract his attention. The name "Cherry" was also heard by a press photographer, who was immediately aware of the identity of the man who was cuddling the bear and was allowed to take photographs. Cherry had to attend an official luncheon. As he left, that afternoon, newsboys were rushing up and down the streets with early editions of the evening papers and "splashed across the front pages were magnificent photographs of myself in the koala bear enclosure."

Wrote Cherry: "The perpetual pageant of amusing and unusual creatures to be found in Australia can best be likened to an All Star show week in London, except that Nature puts on an infinitely more original entertainment than man could ever devise!" He photographed a captive platypus and was told that a full-grown animal could not exist on less than sixteen ounces of worms per day. The diet of that platypus, named Splash, included eggs and grubs.

The kookaburra, or laughing jackass, posed for him and he was told it was respected as the slayer of snakes. "The popularity of the kookaburra is easy to explain, for its funny mannerisms and antics, together with its infectious laughter, endears it to anyone with a spark of humour and imagination." He stalked a female lyre bird in a dark, humid forest and photographed her as she paused in her scratching among the dead leaves. He then managed to get within twenty-five feet of a male and was lucky enough to see him with his tail erect for a few seconds. "For years I had looked forward to this moment – to photograph one of the greatest artists of the feathered world."

Cherry added to his collection pictures of the stump-tailed lizard, giant earth-worm, spiny ant-eater, flying squirrel, emu and, of course, the kangeroo, "a creature which leads a tragic life, when one realizes that in addition to being the victim of Man, it is subjected to the terror of the eagle, which preys on the young joes, and also the dingoes, which hunt in pairs or packs… But a pleasanter picture of its life is visible in the evening, when it can be seen with its family making its way to their favourite feeding-grounds. As dawn breaks, they return home again."

The Keartons visited New Zealand, impressed by the friendliness of its people, the wide variety of scenery and unusual wildlife. In Wellington, he was approached by a young man whose brother lived opposite to Cherry's sister "in a little village in Westmorland." (This was Nateby). In March, 1936, he did a lecture tour and spoke over the radio in studios at Auckland and Wellington. "After my broadcast [at Wellington] that evening, I was greeted by a family of Keartons, who were distant relations, and who had travelled all the way from Napier to meet me. This happy surprise was followed by a friendly and charming meeting with the Yorkshire Society of New Zealand."

Cherry lived too busy a life to spend much time in reflection, yet in his book *Adventures with Animals and Men*, published in 1935 – the year of his visit to the Antipodes – he lamented the decline of wildlife and of the quality of films made of them. Whereas before the Great War, natural history films were a constant wonder to the public and very popular, pioneers such as the Keartons soon had their imitators, who tried to "go one better" than the men they copied.

"As the cinematograph became more popular, its story-telling possibilities ruled it and films which did not tell a story came to be classed as 'educational'." Mammon, in the shape of box-office receipts, triumphed over art. A "sex story" was introduced in a bid for popularity. "So the real natural history film, of which I had been a pioneer, ignominiously died. And with it threatened to go all my work as a natural history kinephotographer."

He was to lament the numerical decline in African wildlife which, on his first acquaintance with what was called the Dark Continent had been profuse and varied. The wholesale extermination of big game was due in part to the settler and in part to "a certain type of photographic expedition or safari which, while pretending to forward the interests of Natural History, frequently takes as big a toll of animal life as the Big Game hunter proper, who goes out with the sole and frank idea of collecting specimens."

Introducing his book *In the Land of the Lion* in 1929 he was concerned at the preservation of the native fauna. "At one time, the title of this book might very well have referred to the whole of Africa, for that was the land of the lion. But civilisation and the lion do not agree and as district after district in Africa has come under civilisation, the lion has gradually died out." Now, with few exceptions, he was to be found in great numbers only in his last and greatest stronghold – Central Africa.

He mentioned the concept of the game reserve, which was not a fenced-in enclosure but a tract of land whose limits were purely geographical and where killing was forbidden. That was not sufficient. Nor was it enough to attempt to limit shooting by the issue of £100 licences permitting only a certain number of victims, for not every man was conscientious. "You will save wildlife only by altering the popular point of view, so that indiscriminate slaughter shall no longer be tolerated."

In 1935, this indomitable man was still producing films about animals and men – wild animals and African tribesmen, not film stars. He reflected: "It has been a long journey from the day when I bought that five-shilling camera in my boyhood to the present time when I am still producing films of animal life; yet all of it has been a grand adventure…"

# Last Rites

RICHARD DIED in 1928, aged 66. He had said to a friend: "If I am as happy in the Other World as I have been in this, I shall be happy indeed." He was facing his third serious illness. One had crippled him as a child. The next forced his retirement to the country.

Fellow dalesmen officiated at the funeral. His cousin, the Rev A W Anderson, described the dead naturalist as having been "a large-hearted, big-souled man… Years ago I heard him lecture and came under the sway of his breezy and bracing personality. Later I read his books and recognised him as a pioneer blazing a trail which others followed."

He recalled the shock of discovering that Richard was lame. "One could not have imagined that the hero of so many exploits on field and fell, by land and sea, at home and abroad, could have been so handicapped. The strength he lost from his crippled limb went into his will. He drove his body for all it was worth."

A writer signing himself T A C, in an obituary tribute to Richard published in *The Manchester Guardian* of February 13, 1928, noted: "Kearton was an artist – his pictures show it – and also a born naturalist. Earlier photographers had obtained pictures of birds but it was Kearton who, by his ingenuity, perfected – even if he did not invent – the "hide" which enabled the artist to work within a few feet of his subject.

"Kearton's hollow cows, sheep and imitation tree-stumps were original and effective: those who to-day use rubbish heaps, haycocks and otherwise camouflaged tents were inspired directly or indirectly by him… Kearton's success stirred many to experiment as well as imitate. Far and wide, in all continents and islands, ornithologists have taken up bird photography and many of them hardly know his name...

"His books, illustrated with his own and his brother's pictures – for he enlisted his brother to help and taught him the art – have had a well-deserved popularity; they may not rank as scientifically complete, but they have served to increase the love, even passion, for nature. He was modest about his scientific attainments and did not profess to be more than a field naturalist. He willingly helped others and showed no jealousy if they had better opportunities of study or produced superior pictures than he was able to obtain...

"The desire to depict birds alive has done more than anything else to combat the wish to possess birds dead. The hope of photographing the bird on the nest has deadened the longing to steal the eggs. Birds at times may suffer from too much photography but they suffer less from the photographer than from the collector. Watching birds, we learn to love and respect them and thus become, like Kearton, keen bird protectors."

In the same column, Francis Heatherley, MB, wrote that Richard was far more than a popular lecturer and writer on natural history subjects. "Among the crowd of photographers who followed in his footsteps the benefit he conferred on us by his inventions is apt to be forgotten." The pioneer work of Richard Kearton had led to "the marvellous nature photographs which now daily meet the eye, whether it be one taken in the eyrie showing the eagle feeding her young, a flashlight photograph of a lion returning to his kill at night or one of a little butterfly asleep in a Surrey garden."

Cherry died just after broadcasting in Children's Hour on BBC radio in 1940. He was aged 68. He was buried at St Mary's, Caterham, and on the grave reposes a memorial of Yorkshire stone in the form of an open book on a greystone slab, with the inscription:

*In loving memory of Cherry Kearton*
*Naturalist and Explorer*
*1871-1940*
*Life is but a sheet of paper white*
*on which each one of us*
*a line or two may write.*
*Then cometh the Light.*

In August, 1943, a tablet of Aberdeen granite in memory of Cherry was unveiled on the outer wall of Muker School, not far from one that commemorated his equally illustrious brother. The memorial to Cherry was provided by his widow, who was then staying in Harrogate. At a church service before the unveiling, the vicar said that Cherry had the faculty of seeing things for himself and making others see them. The work of wildlife recording that began with the Kearton brothers lives in many glorious forms.

Recalling his far-ranging travels, Cherry wrote: "To-day, having encircled the globe several times, and penetrated into many places where no humans have ever been, I can fairly claim to have achieved my schoolboy's dream. And yet to-day I am still far from satisfied and want to start all over again! That is due to Nature's tantalising way of keeping one in suspense, revealing but a few of her wonders at a time and leaving one always wanting to see more."

He added some words by Keble:

*Thou, who hast given me eyes to see*
*And love this sight so fair,*
*Give me a heart to find out Thee,*
*And read Thee everywhere.*

# Appendices

## 1.   The Kearton families

Richard and Ellen had two daughters, Dora and Grace, and three sons, Richard, Cherry and John. Dora's was a breech-birth in 1893; she was a lifelong cripple and died in 1968. Grace, born in 1892, married Howard Bentham in 1921 and had a daughter, Marguerite. Grace died in 1978. Howard predeceased her by ten years.

Richard, born in 1898, married Elizabeth Cobb and had two children, Martin and Primrose. Richard having retained ownership of a field in Swaledale, it passed in due course to Martin and to Primrose, who married Arthur Razzell. Cherry (1902-1989) had three children, Anne, Hilary and Cherry. John (1900-1968) followed in his father's footsteps for a time, photographing natural history and working on the lecture circuit. He wrote two books, *Bird Life in England* and *Nature Memories*.

Cherry, brother of Richard, and a partner in the pioneering photographic work, married Mary Coates in 1900. They had two children. Cherry Edward, born in 1901, married Patience Wood in 1935 and he died in 1977. Morella married Esmond Bulmer. Cherry, snr., had wanderlust. The time spent away from home caused that marriage to fail. He later met Ada Forrest, a celebrated South African singer. They were married in 1922. She gave up her career and followed her husband on many of his expeditions.

## 2. Extracts from Letters written by Richard Kearton to Frank Lowe, of Bolton

*The first letter was from the Royal George Hotel, Knutsford. All succeeding letters from Ashdene, Caterham Valley, Surrey.*

### Feb 19, 1924

As you will see from the above address I am very much on the road. Directly I get a day at home I will look out a print or two and send them for your exhibition. Sorry I cannot say anything about a lecture until I've seen my agent. He's booking me up like steam, although I have asked him to hold his hand until I see how I feel in the spring. I had a bad attack of 'flu a few weeks after I saw you and it has played Old Harry with me and I'm threatening to take a holiday – the first I shall have indulged in for a quarter of a century.

### 24.2.24

For an ordinary slide lecture I will charge you £8.8.0 if I happen to be in your neighbourhood doing other work and if I have to come specially £9.9.0. Please keep these quotations to yourself as far as possible as my usual fee in the North is £10.10.0... If you rope in 400 people there ought to be no fear of making a loss.

### 21.5.24

I confine myself now-a-days to a green and glorified skirt (in point of size) which I place over myself and the camera.

The ideas people express about the field naturalist are very amusing. Opinions about your humble servant are divided. One half the people conclude I'm mad and the other half that I'm making a fortune out of my job. Neither correct, although both expressed with much confidence.

Have ten birds of different species breeding in my gdn and orchard at the present moment. The poor things seem to have a lot of confidence in me and my gun. Last night I shot a monster rat and *very* very nearly a cat. The rascal only just revealed his identity in the nick of time. I saw something stir by a stick heap outside where I have shot several rats lately. I swung the gun on and was just abt to pull when I discovered it was a Cat. Lucky for him!

*20.8.24*

I had to abandon non-flam-films as they were so brittle that a poor projector wrecked them.

*29.8.24.*

Glad to hear you have "just washed up". I have done all that kind of thing myself and admire anyone else who is equal to it. Being a naturalist makes you a natural man.

*28.9.24*

The specialist blamed my few remaining teeth for the neuritis in my throat but the dentist, after three goes of probing, tapping and scraping, says "no". So I have to go and have my lower jaw x rayed.

*12.10.24*

Had a fine audience at Hawes and as the people in the district look upon me as one of their own I had a right royal reception.

*28.10.24*

In regard to coloured slides, I fear I cannot tell you how my wife gets her effects and doubt if she could herself without writing a Volume

about it. She used to be an artist and I suppose that fact has something to do with the effects she produces.

### 29.11.24

I was fairly near you when you wrote – viz., at Nelson, where I
lectured to a crowded house in the evening. Wasn't it a brute of a day?
I went out for a short walk in the morning but I felt wretchedly queer
as I was suffering from another attack of neuritis in my throat. I had
been A1 for a week or two and was just shaking hands with myself
when my enemy suddenly pounced upon me in the train between
Rugby and Crewe on the Saturday. It did not upset my voice at all
but the pain creates such infernal depression that I don't feel fit to go
to a dog's funeral whilst it is on.

   Glad to hear of your success on the platform. Take my advice and
don't lecture for nothing unless it is under very special circumstances.
I did at the beginning and found it did not enhance the value of my
subject or me.

### 17.12.24

I'm just back from Scotland where I finished up for the half season
by talking to 2,000 people in a hall that looked like a forty acre field.

### 23.1.25

Went to Faversham to lecture and stayed with Sir Sidney Alexander.
Talked and lectured from 5 p.m. until 12 a.m. and tired my voice box
out. Shan't accept private hospitality again for a while.

### 23.2.25

Slow motion pictures may be quite good for a scientific demonstration but I do not think much of them for a popular audience and feel

very glad I never spent £400 on a camera to take them. My wife dislikes the things intensely. Moving pictures of any sort have had their day. I have far more demand for slide lectures than movies.

*22.3.25*

I'm just drafting out my autobiography as I sit in ry [sic] trains, hotel lounges and so on. When it sees the light of day, which I hope it will, I feel sure some of it will make you laugh.

*2.7.25*

I am sorry to hear your late partner was too narrow to tolerate Sunday work. I think I have worked on something during every Sunday in my life but, on the other hand, have tried to turn every day in the week into a Sunday. In my boyhood I knew so many people who doffed their religion with their Sunday clothes. It rather disgusted me and I determined to stand up for truth and righteousness without fear of punishment or thirst for reward. Oh! if some of these religious people would only study the great and wonderful acts of Nature they would see what a wee cramped thing they have in their narrowness made of the Great Architect of the Universe.

*5.8.25*

I am very sorry indeed to hear what you say about trade… I do not like the look of things a bit… If I were a young man I should emigrate. I do not say much about it to my boys because their Mother would miss them so much but I think a lot… Don't lecture for nothing. It is as bad to pauperise the mind as the body.

*27.8.25*

I have just been reading Bewick's Life but think mine will be more entertaining. He was a dear chap but far more given to preaching and moralising than I shall be found to be.

*6.9.25*

I don't see any earthly reason why some publisher should not take the little book you mention. Try one but don't put any money down or sell outright. You supply the goods, let the publisher do the work and pay you a 10% royalty. Those are my terms for the little work now in the press but I am paying for some extra pictures out of my royalty.

   Sorry to say I am not feeling better. Went to see a specialist last Tuesday and he has knocked me off everything I like but my pipe. Work, fish, flesh, fowl, tea, coffee, &c. Blood pressure bad and I feel as weak as an old hen that has sat for a month on rotten eggs. Luckily Jack [John, his son] is able to take over some of my work.

*30.7.26*

When the British working man has been schooled into admitting that he is only $^2/_3$ the man his father was, and is prepared to accept charity from people much worse off than he is, I reckon he has been reduced to the position of a louse…

*3.10.26*

All the swallows, martins and chiff chaffs appear to have gone. I expect the cold snap sent them away in a hurry. The weather here is at the moment glorious. A fortnight ago I spent a few days with an old doctor friend down in Kent. Did a bit of fishing and caught 12 perch and 2 roach.

*23.6.27*

I think you have made quite a good bag in Texel. I found the

Dutchmen quite a delightful lot and they were all most kind to me. I'm glad to hear they have treated you so well. What have the Englishmen done to incur the displeasure of the Dutchmen? I expect it is the Egg Collector again, trying to accomplish his dirty ends by posing as a photographer.

I hope to be at my old home in Swaledale during August and if I get over to see some of my relatives near Burnley will certainly drop in and see you and some dear old friends at Bury.

*8.8.27*

Take my advice and don't bother your head about D & W. I have never seen either of them and am never likely to do so. I have made it a point in my life never to judge any man by the other fellow's story and in old age have come to the conclusion that life is not long enough to bother about upsets. Stick to wild nature and go steadily on your own path.

I tried my hand at fishing for trout in Yorks last summer but the fish were either too highly educated or my hand had lost its cunning.

*Dec 7, 27*

Are you sure the fool Collier shot a Gt Northern Diver? I have never seen this bird on fresh water and suspect that many people confuse the Black Throated Diver with it. Get a look at the skin if the bird is being stuffed locally. If I had my way I would have more restrictions on guns and gunners.

I am afraid I cannot supply what you ask in regard to birds in the Highlands. I got my Crested Tit on Speyside and Capercaillie in Perth but don't remember the name of a keeper at either place as it is so long ago. The only two pictures I have for sale are a couple of photogravures (1) A fox sitting outside his earth (2) A group of young Song Thrushes on a branch. Of these I only have a few copies and they will soon be advertised in the *Countryside* at a bob each including Autograph. Far too cheap but I want to clear them out.

*9.12.27.*

Many thanks for your kind letter of the 7th inst and box of Health Builder, which I am going to try at once. Like you I am not much of a believer in physic but am convinced that anything calculated to help the body to defend itself against its numerous foes is a distinct benefit... You will be sorry to learn that a builder has just commenced the ripping up of the lovely hanger behind Ashdene. I suppose one ought not to be selfish but it seems a pity to destroy one of the prettiest bits of country round London.

# 3. Books written by the Kearton brothers

**1890** *Birds' Nests, Eggs and Egg-Collecting.* R Kearton, FZS. Illustrated with 22 coloured plates. Cassell.

**1897** *With Nature and a Camera.* Richard Kearton FZS, FRPS & Cherry Kearton. Cassell. Dedicated "to the memory of our beloved father and mother, who now lie sleeping where the rock thrush pipes his lonesome note and the moorcock becks at dawn of day."

**1898** *Wild Life at Home: How to Study and Photograph It*, R Kearton FZS. Illustrated by photographs taken direct from Nature by C Kearton. Cassell. Dedicated "to a host of dear old comrades toiling within sound of the beloved hum of Fleet Street".

**1899** *Our Rarer British Breeding Birds: Their Nests, Eggs and Summer Haunts*, by Richard Kearton FZS. With Illustrations from Photographs by C Kearton. Cassell. To be regarded as a supplement to our former work on *British Birds' Nests: How Where and When to find and Identify Them*, published in 1895.

**1901** *Strange Adventures in Dicky-bird Land: Stories told by Mother Birds to Amuse their Chicks.* Overheard by R Kearton FZS and illustrated from photos by C Kearton. Cassell.

**1902** *The Natural History of Selborne, by Gilbert White.* With notes by R Kearton, FZS, FRPS, and numerous illustrations by Cherry and Richard Kearton. Cassell.

**1905** *The Adventures of Cock Robin. And his Mate*, by R Kearton, FZS, with upwards of 120 illustrations from photographs taken direct from Nature by Cherry and Richard Kearton. Cassell.

**1907** *The Fairy-Land of Living Things*, Richard Kearton, FZS. Illustrated from photographs taken direct from wild free nature by Cherry Kearton. Cassell.

**1909** *Our Bird Friends: a Book for all Boys and Girls*, Richard Kearton, FZS, with one hundred original illustrations from photographs by C Kearton. Cassell. Dedicated to "the little naturalist who tried to catch a wily old sparrow with a pinch of salt."

**1911** *The Nature-Lover's Handbook*, Richard Kearton, FZS, FRPS, and others. Cassell.

**1911** *The Adventures of Jack Rabbit*. Richard Kearton, FZS, FRPS. With eight autochromes and numerous photographs direct from Nature by Richard and Grace Kearton. Cassell.

**1912** *Baby Birds at Home*. Richard Kearton, FZS, Etc. With four colour plates and sixty illustrations from photographs by Cherry and Grace Kearton. Cassell.

**1913** *Wild Life Across the World*, Cherry Kearton. The fourth impression, which is undated, though has the 1930s style, includes a note by the publisher, Arrowsmith, indicating that the present volume, containing about two-thirds of the material included in the original, is now re-written and carefully edited, together with new records of Mr Kearton's more recent experiences. The dedication is "to the memory of my dear friend Theodore Roosevelt."

Another undated edition of this book, published by Hodder and Stoughton, has an introduction by Theodore Roosevelt, in which he states that Cherry and his brother had long been identified with the remarkable work of nature photography. Not only had Cherry been a pioneer in this work, but he had done more than any other man to aid its development. "I have long followed the extraordinary work of the Kearton Brothers in photographing English birds… Later I met Mr Cherry Kearton in Africa and there saw him at work." One of the prime qualities of Kearton's work was its "absolute trustworthiness." His photographs were of truly wild animals pictured in the precise circumstances he described.

**1915** *Wonders of Wild Nature*, Richard Kearton, FZS, FRPS, etc. With 72 Photographs direct from Nature by the Author and his Daughter, Grace Kearton. Cassell. The book is notable in that it bears a date in the Great War and several of the pictures are reproduced in colour.

**1922** *At Home With Nature*, by Richard Kearton FZS., etc. Profusely illustrated with Photographs taken direct from Nature by Captain Cherry Kearton and the Author. Cassell.

**1923** *Wild Birds Adventures: A Nature Story Book for Boys and Girls*, Richard Kearton, FZS, &c. Illustrated from Photographs taken Direct from Nature by the Author. Cassell.

**1924** *The Shifting Sands of Algeria*. Cherry Kearton. With 79 photographs. Arrowsmith. Dedicated to "my friend T Walrond Innes."

**1925** *My Friend Toto*. The Adventures of a Chimpanzee and the Story of his Journey from the Congo to London. Told by Cherry Kearton. With a preface by Sir Gilbert Parker. And 22 photographs by the author. Arrowsmith.

**1926** *A Naturalist's Pilgrimage*, Richard Kearton FZS. With eight plates. Cassell. Dedicated "to My Little Wife… in gratitude for immeasurable help and sympathy during our long pull in double harness."

*My Dog Simba.* The Adventures of a Fox-Terrier. Cherry Kearton. With 21 photographs by the author. Arrowsmith.

1927 *My Happy Family.* The Adventures of Mary the Chimpanzee and The Story of her Friendship with a Fox-Terrier and a Mongoose, told by Cherry Kearton. With 23 photographs by the author. Arrowsmith.

1928 *My Animal Friendships.* The Adventures of Timmy the Rat, Chuey the Cheetah, Robin Parker the Mongoose, Mr Penguin, Jane the Elephant and Mrs Spider. Told by Cherry Kearton. With 20 photographs by the author. Arrowsmith.

1929 *In the Land of the Lion,* by Cherry Kearton, with 88 photographs. Dedicated "to Ada my wife". Sixth impression published by Arrowsmith.

1930 *The Island of Penguins,* Cherry Kearton. With forty-six photographs and a map. Longmans, Green. Dedicated "to the memory of Dick, my dear brother and comrade over many rough roads."

1932 *The Animals Came to Drink,* Cherry Kearton. With 42 photographs by the author. Longmans, Green & Co.

1934 *The Lion's Roar,* Cherry Kearton. With 38 photographs by the author. Longmans, Green & Co.

1935 *Adventures with Animals and Men,* Cherry Kearton. With 44 photographs by the author. Longmans, Green and Co. Includes an illuminating chapter on Cherry's development as a nature photographer.

1937 *I Visit the Antipodes,* Cherry Kearton. With 68 illustrations. Jarrolds Publishers. Dedicated to Captain Cook.

**1938** *My Woodland Home*, Cherry Kearton. With 81 illustrations. Jarrolds.

**1941** *Cherry Kearton's Travels*, by Cherry Kearton. Illustrated by photographs taken by the author. Robert Hale.

## Two Books by John Kearton
(Richard's son)

**1931** *Bird Life in England*, John Kearton. With forty-eight illustrations. Philip Allan.

**1950** *Nature Memories*, John Kearton. With 78 illustrations. Jarrolds. The style of this book is, as the title implies, richly anecdotal, as were those of his father and uncle. He deals with quirky aspects of natural history, such as why the dormouse is called the "whistling mouse" and "the manner in which Nature's bulldozer, the Mole, blighted the hopes of a Partridge."

# 4.   Some Personal Glimpses

*From "Giggleswick Chronicle" No 93. 17 December, 1910:*

Mr Kearton [Richard] paid a second visit to the School on November 10th and lectured on *Wild Birds and Beasts at Home.* Mr Kearton has devoted his life to the study of British Birds and Beasts and their habitats. The result is a most valuable record of facts and an extraordinarily interesting collection of photographs. Mr Kearton migrates with the birds: he leaves his Surrey home and works his way gradually north with the Spring, assuming all manner of disguises, for Man is still the Bird's worst foe. Sometimes the guise is a reversible coat of different shades of green, sometimes a stone cairn or the skin of the homely cow.

The value of photography in solving Nature's riddles is enormous; it proves indubitably to the eye that certain things firmly held by some naturalists and equally firmly refuted by others really do exist. To give a single instance: it has long been asserted by naturalists that the Kestrel Hawk does not build its own nest but seizes that of some other bird. Mr Kearton showed us photographs which prove that this is not always the case.

*Comments by Charles Davy on the screening of "The Big Game of Life" at the Polytechnic Theatre, London, April, 1935:*

Here is a new method of autobiography. Mr Cherry Kearton, the famous animal photographer, tells the story of his life in moving pictures, taken mostly by himself through the last thirty years. The films are silent, with Mr Kearton acting as commentator throughout; his commentary is quiet and straightforward, happily free from facetious smartness.

The effect of so many short extracts, loosely strung together, is bound to be scrappy; and I could not quite avoid the rather tired feeling that comes when someone is sitting at your side and flicking over the pages of a snapshot album. You have hardly time to focus your attention on a herd of giraffes before you are watching hippopotamuses at a drinking pool – and so on. I should have preferred fewer and longer extracts; but there are many vivid and sometimes exciting studies of wild creatures of every kind; and some delightful views of African piccaninnies.

*"Yorkshire Evening News", August, 1935:*

Rarely a year has passed for a considerable time without Mrs Kearton coming to take the cure at Harrogate. There is another reason why she is so pleased to return. She enjoyed many concert triumphs there in the days when she was known as Miss Ada Forrest, the South African soprano. Cherry Kearton told me: "I often think of the days when I trod along the Buttertubs, the rocky expanse between Hawes and Swaledale, and of my schooldays at Muker. I am going along to Muker this week-end to see the graves of my parents and to visit old relatives and friends."

Mr Kearton's visit to Yorkshire has coincided with the trade presentation in Leeds of his new film *The Big Game of Life* and he put in a personal appearance. There are introductory "shots" of his birthplace on the Yorkshire moorlands and then follow his first balloon flight over London, his early experiments with a 5s camera and his subsequent travels in Central Africa and Borneo.

*In the "Yorkshire Post", April, 1936:*

"First" is a great word with Mr Kearton. He published the first photographically illustrated bird book in the world. In 1903 he took the first motion-pictures of a wild bird – and, oddly enough, it was in the fields round Elstree that he made his early shots. The clatter of the primitive camera increased his difficulties, till he contrived to deaden it with a casing of sawdust and felt – a means of insulation which he found still in use when he lately visited one of our big film studios.

In Africa, he flew in the first aeroplane to appear there and showed East Africa the first film of its own fauna. In 1906 he took the first aerial pictures over London – a perilous adventure, for at the start the erratic dirigible soared to 14,000 feet and was presently wrecked. Mr Kearton hopes before long to show his latest film, *The Big Game of Life*, in his native Swaledale, where some of it was made.

*"Yorkshire Post", April, 1938:*

Mr Cherry Kearton tells us in his intimate style of a Yorkshire horse that developed a taste for beer …in his latest book, *My Woodland Home*. It is inevitable that in any book he writes, Cherry Kearton should relate some reminiscences, no matter how trivial, of his native Yorkshire. He was born at Thwaite in Swaledale. One recalls, with a glow of pride, while sitting on a garden seat at Harrogate, he described some years ago the small farm his father kept; how he and his famous brother Richard studied birds and animals in Swaledale.

The latest book of Mr Kearton's appears to have been conceived, not not actually written, at Harrogate. He began thinking of happy days of long ago when he rose at 4 a.m. and tramped the country lanes to capture Nature studies. In his book he relates that "as a boy in the Yorkshire Dales I well remember one particular horse developing a taste for beer. We had four haytime scythe-mowers at work and in those days beer was provided for the men in stone, wicker-covered bottles.

"To keep the liquid cool, it was laid under the newly-mown swathe, which is the line of grass cut down by the mowers. Now, immediately the horse entered the field, he would start to search for the beer, up and down the swathes, and would not cease until he had discovered one of the bottles. Then, in a very short time, he had the cork out and was enjoying the contents, that is, if it was nearly full, for as the bottle fell sideways the beer naturally spilled out."

*From "Darlington and Stockton Times," March, 1956:*

*Punch* said of Cherry Kearton, "No man has seen so many animals since the days of Noah." He preferred a camera to a gun and secured many notable records of Nature at its wildest. He last visited Swaledale in 1934 to make the opening sequences of a film of his life story, *The Big Game of Life.*

Mrs Cherry Kearton, widow of the Swaledale-born naturalist, has written a book of reminiscences, *On Safari* which she discussed on TV in Saturday's "In Town Tonight" feature. Daughter of the late Mr and Mrs James Forrest, she was born in Natal and studied at the Royal Academy of Music. Meeting Cherry on board ship after he had given a talk on wild life photography, she married him.

Abandoning her singing career, she took on the business side of his life even giving him a hand with the camera. Asked by the BBC compere on Saturday to recall any exciting moments in her life, she had this to say:

"We were driving through a wooded part of Zululand when Cherry touched my arm and pointed to a huge white rhino. Rhinos cannot see more than 15 yards and depend on sound and scent for direction. Fortunately the wind was blowing from the rhino to us and the animal had no idea of our presence. Cherry walked 20 yards towards the rhino and when he was 12 yards from it, the rhino raised its head, gave a terrible snort and charged."

Mrs Kearton confessed that at that moment she dropped her head and closed her eyes in fear, her heart throbbing wildly. "This is the end," she thought. "When I opened my eyes," she continued, "there was Cherry walking calmly towards me with his camera and there was the rhino disappearing in the distance. It appears the rhinos have a dislike of buzzing sounds such as that produced by a cine-camera and so the would-be attacker made off."

*From the "Yorkshire Post" in 1962, the centenary year of Richard Kearton's birth:*

Little has changed in lonely Thwaite in the 100 years. The four-roomed farm cottage known as Corner House, where the brothers were born, is still there, occupied by Mr J G Reynoldson and his family. "Every summer," said Mr Reynoldson, "we get people standing in the yard and looking at the old place. The Keartons made Corner House famous." There are still Keartons living in Thwaite – three brothers who are sons of a cousin of Richard and Cherry. One brother, who lives at Moor Close Farm, bears the name of Cherry Kearton.

Eighty-year-old Mr David Harker, an old school chum of Cherry, is still living at Muker. "Cherry was a rum lad," he said. "Always had his breeches backside hanging out, for the family were very poor. We had some fun and sometimes got into trouble. But he was a sharp lad and a very brave one…" To the end of their lives, Richard and Cherry paid frequent visits to Muker to stay with the Harkers. "Now only Mrs Cherry Kearton is alive," said Mrs Harker. "She lives in London but we hear from her frequently."

Cherry escaped death and disaster a score of times and died on the steps of Broadcasting House in 1940, after giving a talk on Children's Hour. Said David Harker: "I heard those last words on my radio in Muker. I didn't know until next morning that I had said farewell to Cherry Kearton."

# Castleberg Books

*by the same author*

| | |
|---|---:|
| Birds of the Lake District | £6.50 |
| Birds of the Yorkshire Dales | £6.50 |
| Ghost-hunting in the Yorkshire Dales | £5.99 |
| Music of the Yorkshire Dales | £5.99 |
| Cuckoo Town – Dales Life in the 1950's | £6.50 |
| Sacred Places of the Lake District | £6.50 |
| Beatrix Potter – Her Life in the Lake District | £6.20 |
| The Lost Village of Mardale | £5.60 |
| One Hundred Tales of the Settle-Carlisle Railway | £6.99 |
| The Story of Ribblehead Viaduct | £5.50 |
| How They Built the Settle-Carlisle Railway | £5.50 |
| Garsdale – History of a Junction Station | £6.50 |
| Mile by Mile on the Settle to Carlisle | £5.99 |
| The Men Who Made the Settle to Carlisle | £5.99 |
| | |
| Life in the Lancashire Milltowns | £5.99 |
| | |
| Nobbut Middlin' | £6.99 |
| Nowt's Same | £6.50 |
| You're Only Old Once | £5.99 |

*Mini biographies:*

| | |
|---|---:|
| Edward Elgar in the Yorkshire Dales | £4.99 |
| Fred Taylor – Yorkshire Cheesemaker | £4.99 |
| Tot Lord and the Bone Caves | £4.50 |
| Edith Carr – Life on Malham Moor | £4.50 |

Orders to **Kingfisher Productions**, 'Felmersham', Mills Road,
Osmington Mills, Weymouth, Dorset DT3 6HE
Tel & Fax 01305 832906   www.railwayvideo.com

*All post free in the UK. £2.50 per item overseas.*
*Please allow 28 days for delivery, although we do endeavour to*
*send on the day of receiving the order.*